The BILLIONAIRE

The Continuum

PETRA NICOLL

LUMINARE PRESS

WWW.LUMINAREPRESS.COM

The Billionaire: The Continuum
© 2017 Petra Nicoll

Printed in the United States of America

Cover Design: Claire Flint Last

Luminare Press
438 Charnelton St., Suite 101
Eugene, OR 97401
www.luminarepress.com

LCCN: 2017958913
ISBN: 978-1-944733-49-0

CHAPTER ONE

GOOD MORNING, BANGKOK

Derek Stryker rooted his head firmly against the seatback of a plush recliner in his company's Boeing 722 jet. He was used to sleeping on planes. The narrow yet spacious expanse offered him both a comfortable office and an area for relaxation; a calm respite from his normal fast-paced life.

He'd left his home in Connecticut nearly fifteen hours before. He was pleased with what he'd accomplished enflight and looked forward to rewarding himself once he settled into his hotel room. For now, he would try to get some sleep before his arrival.

It was a few hours later when his rest was interrupted, "Mr. Stryker?" A gentle tap on his shoulder jarred him awake. "I'm sorry, Mr. Stryker, but the plane will be landing shortly."

Derek looked up at the flight attendant—a young Thai girl who often serviced this leg of his travels. His vision was a bit cloudy, as the last three hours had not been enough to sleep off the four bourbons he'd consumed during the flight. The attendant's warning signaled it was time to begin his routine. He pulled his seat forward and turned on the air above his head, letting the cold air blast upon his face.

Taking a deep breath, he stepped carefully but confidently from his seat to the bathroom, where he washed his face with his favorite Caswell Massey bath soap and cold water. He took one quick glance at his reflection in the mirror, appreciating how impressive he still looked at fifty years old. He had inherited his father's thick head of blonde hair, which blended subtly with the gray around his perfectly-trimmed sideburns.

Returning to his seat, his triple espresso and orange juice were waiting for him, and he drank each of them in turn in one big swig.

"Please take your seat, Mr. Stryker, in preparation for landing." The pilot's voice came through over the loudspeaker. Captain Cooper worked exclusively for Derek; he was well-compensated for the frenetic schedule that was often expected of him. "The temperature in Bangkok is a comfortable eighty-three degrees. We are arriving on time at the local hour of 9:50 a.m."

Derek let out a small sigh. "Good," he thought. He hated being late.

In a few minutes, he stepped off the plane. His porter carried his briefcase and managed his Tumi rollaway luggage. Everything else he needed would be waiting for him at his hotel upon arrival; it would have been impractical to bring the heavy cotton clothes he wore in the U.S. to Thailand. The humidity immediately hit his whole body, and within minutes the clothes he was wearing felt damp and sweaty.

He quickly cleared customs and, in response to the text message he'd received from his driver, continued directly to curbside pickup. Ashok was there waiting for him, the door to his white limousine already ajar. Derek took off his Armani linen jacket and strode toward the limo.

"Welcome back to Bangkok, sir," the Indian driver gestured for Derek to enter the vehicle. Derek took his seat inside—the furthest in the back, passenger-side. Ashok had been working for Derek for many years—since Derek's father had been alive and owned the Grand Palace Hotel, to which the two men were now headed. It was a twenty-minute drive from the airport, and it was a route Ashok could practically make blindfolded.

The hotel belonged to Derek now, as one of the many inheritances from his father. Another was Stryker Industries, a conglomerate of sky-rise building companies, together with steel and other foreign investments. Derek was pleased his net worth was close to forty billion at this point—a figure that impressed him but did not stop him from trying to surpass.

He entered the lobby of the hotel; its entrance was opulent, yet tastefully refined. Derek approached the front desk and was immediately offered a leather-bound menu. A room key was also handed to him, for his usual private luxury suite on the top floor of the hotel. "I trust your choice remains the same as discussed?" the concierge asked.

"It does." Derek slipped five 100 dollar bills inside and closed the menu, handing it back to the concierge.

"For your efforts."

"Thank you very much, sir. Your massage therapists will be up shortly."

"No, not just yet. Another couple of hours and I'll be ready." He wanted to take a proper nap and a shower first.

"As you wish."

Derek continued to his room, anxious to sleep off the

ill-effects of his flight so that his senses may be fully alert to enjoy the best of Bangkok.

Precisely two hours later, two young Thai girls knocked lightly on Derek Stryker's door before entering. Niko stood less than five feet tall, no more than ninety pounds. She was a beauty. She was heavily made up, but a natural allure shown through her eyes. Her hair was shiny and so sleek that the black rubber band holding her ponytail was sliding down, causing loose strands to frame Niko's delicate face. Her hazel-brown, almond-shaped eyes revealed a battle between fear and determination.

The sound of running water could be heard, as Niko and her older sister, Mona, took their places standing at the foot of the bed. Derek was out of earshot finishing his shower, although it wouldn't have mattered because he spoke no more in Thai than a few words of greeting and narrow business acumen.

"Remember," Mona turned to her sister and whispered in her native tongue, "You must follow through with this. We need the money!"

Niko wouldn't make eye contact with her sister. Her knees had been shaking since she'd woken up at 4 a.m. that morning. Her hands were cool, and her palms glistened with sweat. She remembered them now and wiped them on her black silk skirt. She was certain they would not make a good impression as they were.

She glanced down at her chest. Her breasts were small. They would be barely visible beneath her peach silk blouse, save for the bra her sister had given her that made them appear ampler. The high heels she wore did little to hide her youth. She was a virgin; but having just begun menstruation, she was considered an appropriate age to begin working.

Mona, at nineteen, had been working for nearly six years now. It was her duty as Niko's oldest sister to teach her what was expected of her.

"It won't last long, Niko. The first time never does." She paused before adding, "Stop trembling. He will be out soon." Just then the girls heard the steady stream of water come to a stop. Derek stepped out of the shower, reaching for his towel. The bathroom door was only slightly ajar, but it was wide enough for the girls to hear his voice and for Derek to catch their image in the mirror.

"Undress and wait by the bed. I'll be with you in a moment."

Derek poured himself a glass of Dom Perignon and took a sip. He took an ice-cold shower, but the effects of it were notwithstanding. He'd known the menu would include these two girls today. He'd been told about Niko some weeks ago, and the hotel had saved her for him. "So long as you pay for her sister, too," he'd been told.

The older girl was not of much interest to him. She stood tall, with raven black hair down to her waist. She was beautiful, no doubt. But her presence was calm and all-knowing. She didn't leave much mystery to him because he knew he left none for her.

The young girl, however... she tried to hide her fear, but it was plastered on her every pore; and in the way, her gaze hung just off the tip of her nose. Her shoulders leaned slightly down and inward not only because she was timid, but because she seemed to be trying to cover the fact that she had small breasts. For her, what was to come was unknown. He relished that sensation.

Watching the girls undress through the bathroom mirror,

he was pleased with what he saw. Niko was smaller than what he'd expected, both in stature and in development. Her bra slipped easily off her shoulders and down to her waist. Together with her skirt, she let them drop to the floor. She bent over deliberately, her back now turned toward the bathroom, as she slid her panties off and over one foot at a time.

Her hips were narrow, as were her calves, which were not yet defined even with the assistance of heels. Derek had imagined what her thighs looked like. He'd run his fingers up and down them, up and down, as he'd drifted to sleep on his flight earlier. In his mind, he'd stopped before his fingers reached the outer folds of her labia, only because he'd wanted to have a fresh experience of the girl in the flesh.

The moment was finally near. He entered the bedroom, his towel wrapped around his waist. "Come," he motioned to Niko. He sat down on the side of the bed. Mona hung back by the window. They were on the nineteenth floor, and there was no risk of anyone seeing inside, but the curtains were nevertheless drawn.

"How old are you, girl?"

Mona did not allow Niko the chance to answer. "She's seventeen, sir."

"Don't lie to me. How old?'

"She is twelve, sir."

Derek nodded in approval. "Turn around."

Niko stood motionless before sensing urgency from her sister's presence. Mona would only intercede if the client appeared unhappy. She released her clasped hands along her side and did a careful turn.

Now he could take a closer look at her. Her skin was flawless; he could not find even a subtle mark. Its olive tones felt not only exotic to him but transparent—like he could see inside of her.

Inside of her. He let his thoughts linger on the idea. He moved his gaze to her neckline, so as not to get distracted too early. She was removing her jewelry now—the pearls that were far too lavish for practically any girl her age that was not in the business. She'd been groomed for this day.

Derek painted a semi-circle around her neckline with his tongue, enjoying the flavor of citrus from a fragrance she wore that melted deliciously with the salt of her skin. He could feel her heart beating rapidly beneath her chest. He placed his hand over her left breast, "Shhh," he whispered.

Secretly he loved her anxiety, but he wanted her to relax enough to be able to do what he wanted with her. Niko appeared promising. She responded dutifully to her sister's presence and heeded his requests with practiced familiarity. She had seen her sister work before and acted as though she already knew what she had to do.

She reached for Derek without being asked. He'd been ready since stepping out of the shower. Niko lowered to her knees, allowing Derek's hands to embrace either side of her head. He was not gentle, but he was not rough—a hold firm enough to let her know who was in control, but relaxed enough to encourage her to explore as she wished.

One of her hands embraced his testicles as the other stroked the underside of his penis, from the base to the tip, down and back.

She lowered her mouth onto him, as Derek's hands took a slightly stronger grip of her head. As she moved her mouth back and forth, faster and a little faster, Derek began to fear he wouldn't be able to hold out long enough for the premium he paid to be worth it. He pulled out of her mouth abruptly.

He was embarrassed that he had already nearly cum, but that was an emotion he would never admit to himself and especially not to these young girls. Instead, he forced his embarrassment into anger, raising his voice to a level that startled Niko and demanded between slightly ground teeth, "Get on the bed."

She obeyed, diligently. He raised her by the hips and sat her straddled on top of him and did not wait for permission. Her faced winced, and one solitary tear fell from her cheek, but she did not cry out. Moments later, Derek released her from on top of him, lifting her pelvis over slightly to see the blood on the sheets.

"That will be all."

Niko and Mona gathered their clothes and bowed to Derek, whose eyes did not look away from the ceiling. The two exited as swiftly as they'd come.

Derek lay quietly, but not peacefully, behind on the bed. He was never fully satisfied.

Later that evening, Derek successfully closed the deal he'd flown to Bangkok to solidify. He did so the same as always—with charismatic grace, confidence, and lavish gifts. The meeting had been held in the hotel board room on the second floor, with three businessmen—one from China, one from England and another from the U.S. The men had discussed plans for another hotel and a condo complex in downtown Bangkok.

Such deals had become so routine to Derek, that minimal effort was required beyond a commanding presence, a firm handshake, and the customary reward—three menus had been obtained from the hotel concierge that were handed to the men as gifts.

Petra Nicoll

"You will enjoy doing business here, gentlemen." Derek winked and excused himself promptly to take a call from his youngest daughter, Katherine.

Katherine was in Senegal, having recently embarked on a two-year stint working for the Peace Corps. For the life of him, he could not understand why someone would choose to live in a tent in a poverty-stricken country, building…latrines?! But that was his daughter… she did everything opposite of what those in her family had done before her.

"Hi, Dad!"

"Hi, Katherine. How is life down in the trenches?"

Katherine rolled her eyes but simply said, "Fine, Dad. How are you?"

"I am fine. I am in Bangkok, just closed a deal."

"You're always working, Dad."

"That's not true. Sometimes I'm fighting with your mother."

Katherine failed to see any humor in his attempt to change the subject. "I know it's bad, Dad. You know that's why I left, right? I cannot handle all of the dysfunction of Mom." Derek's silence prompted her to continue. "Monique and Thomas act like I'm their therapist. I'm tired of hearing about it. I'm tired of Mom not changing. It's only gotten worse. She's been on methadone pain cocktails ever since we were little, and now there's never a moment when she's not messed up."

"Have you talked to your brother and sister?"

"I'm in Africa, Dad. I'm trying to pretend they don't exist. Thomas is a dry drunk who gets every girl in his path pregnant. I refuse to admit he's my brother. How many houses and opportunities have you offered him, Dad? He has no gratitude for anything you've ever given him. He spent all the money you gave him in college on opiates."

Katherine felt empowered to speak her mind, with countries between them. "And Monique—she's no better. They both hate you for leaving us alone with Mom so much growing up, and they're determined to pay you back for it. Do you remember when Mom would lock us out of the house, and we had to sleep in the pool house because she didn't want us to mess up our beds and the perfect carpet lines? Monique and Thomas blame you for that."

"Why don't you blame me, then? If I messed up so bad, why do you still call me, when my other children ignore me?"

"You were different with me, Dad. You always came to my gymnastics meets. You never missed one." There was a pause of silence on the phone that to Derek lasted uncomfortably long.

Katherine had always been his favorite child. He'd been captivated by her beauty since birth. She'd reminded him of Margaret before she'd gotten ill; she had the same blue eyes, strawberry blonde hair, and feisty spirit. He always thought she should be a model—he could have gotten her on the cover of Vanity Fair had she wanted—but Katherine preferred to study economics. She was more interested in third-world countries than the luxuries she'd grown up with. She was not only beautiful but smart, and he admired her for that.

Derek finally mumbled, "Mmm hmm. Well, you were good. I was proud of you."

Katherine hoped the fact that tears were starting to form would not show through in her voice. "I can't go back there, Dad. I'm going to stay in Africa with the Peace Corp for as long as they'll have me."

"I will jump on the plane in a few weeks and come visit you, okay?"

Petra Nicoll

"Please don't do that, Dad. You'll never understand why I'm living like this. Call Mom instead. She needs to hear from you. She still loves you, you know. Maybe it will help her. I don't know."

"Take care of yourself and be careful, Katherine. Call me if you need anything. I can get you out of there in a heartbeat."

"Go home, Dad."

"I am. First thing in the morning."

"Bye. I love you."

"I love you, too." Derek held the phone to his ear for another thirty seconds before he placed it back in the pocket of his shirt and returned to his room for a drink.

DEREK FUMBLED WITH HIS KEYS AS HE WALKED UP TO THE front door of his Connecticut estate. The grounds were expansive and well kept; he'd never known what it was like to lift a finger to maintain the property, nor had he ever given it any thought. He was always certain of his expectations, however, and they almost always fell short.

Maria, his maid, greeted him at the door. "Welcome home, Mr. Stryker."

Derek placed his briefcase inside the door, tossing that morning's edition of the New York Times on the bureau with his right hand while loosening his tie with his left. His butler would tend to his luggage.

"Where's my wife?" Derek almost mumbled the words. In truth, he didn't care, but he remembered he had a benefit to attend that night, and it was standard protocol for spouses to be there. He recalled the rage he'd felt during the fight they'd had just before he left for Bangkok, though he couldn't even remember what it was about anymore.

More than anything, he just needed to know that his wife was sober and wouldn't make a fool out of him that night. As much as he had grown to despise her, divorce was not an option. He knew she'd never agreed to it for one, and two, he needed her to pull off the family-man image he was careful to protect.

"I don't know, sir. I think at the spa?"

"Mmm," Derek barely registered the maid's response. He was already on his way upstairs to take a shower. It was always the first thing he did when he came home. That, and check his face in the mirror as if to assure himself he was still who he thought he was.

He knew he was living a double life, but he didn't think about it quite that way—more as if he were playing multiple characters in a play. One character was found by a segment of his business network to be a most admirable entrepreneur; he was known for making sharp, seemingly impulsive decisions that marked his boldness and complete disinterest in political correctness. He didn't care about whose toes he might step on. This character cared only about his own agenda. If one happened to share his agenda, he would saddle up next to him as his white knight.

If one's values happened to be in opposition to his, well, then Derek was a disgusting, disturbing, self-serving bigot. He didn't think he really was this character, but he had fun playing him. That's why he enjoyed his trips to Bangkok so much. This last trip had ended differently, though. His daughter's call had thrown him off. She'd forced him to remember details of the past that he'd rather have kept buried.

It's true. He wasn't there for his family. He didn't know how to be—his father never was. At least his children were raised by their mother. He had been raised by nannies. But damn if he didn't give his children everything he knew how to give, he thought. They had pool parties with celebrity performers for their birthdays, each a Rolls Royce at the age of sixteen, tuition for the most prestigious of universities. He even got Thomas into college, God dammit. There's no way his grades would have gotten him past community college on their own, Derek recalled. Still, his children were never satisfied. And they blamed him?! Now he remembered what the fight with his wife had been about before his trip. She had blamed him for her addiction. What a bitch. He was sorry he'd ever married her.

Just then he heard his wife's typical dramatic entrance, "I'm baaack. Maria! I swear to God I'm going replace you with some new Peruvian girl if I have to tell you one more time not to leave the mop leaning up against the wall like that! I can't have those germs getting on the wall."

"Yes, Ma'am. I'm sorry."

She must have been shopping. He could hear the rustle of bags being dropped on the floor as she demanded, "Maria, put these things away. But finish the floors first. I can't handle all this dust in here."

Margaret made her way up the winding staircase to the bedroom. "Oh! You're here," she jumped slightly upon seeing Derek, who was laying back on the bed with his feet planted on the floor, still fully dressed. A wave of unexpected exhaustion had come over him, stalling his plan for a shower.

"Yes, I'm here. But by all means, don't let me stop you from your afternoon fix. I know you keep it in your bedside drawer. " Derek didn't even look up.

"I don't know what you're talking about," Margaret feigned disinterest. "How was Thailand?"

"Thailand was Thailand."

Margaret understood more about what that meant than he realized. "Fix yourself up, Derek. The benefit is in just a few hours, and I can smell pussy on you from here."

Derek opened his mouth slightly; he was about to object but thought better of it. He was too tired for another fight. Instead, he asked, "Have you heard from Thomas or Monique?"

"You know they don't talk to me anymore."

He knew. But he was feeling almost sentimental after his talk with Katherine. Almost, but not quite.

Margaret was in the master bathroom now, but Derek could see the full sight of her in the mirror. All the plastic surgeries she'd had couldn't cover the years of substance abuse she'd put her body through. God, she used to be so beautiful. When they'd met in college, he swore he could forget every other woman if he just had her. And he did, for a while. But then everything changed.

It had all started when they lost their first child to SIDS at two months old. Margaret started on pain cocktails soon after, and before long she was addicted. He thought that once they had another child, everything would go back to how it was. But that wasn't the case. Instead, it was as if Margaret resented all three of their children for the attention they took away from her—which, if he were to be honest, wasn't much. The more the business grew, the less he was home.

And that's when the parties started. She could always smell the alcohol and sex on him when he came home late at night—if he came home at all. He tried to wash it out, but even a shower couldn't cover for him. One night, she felt she couldn't take it any longer. It was 3 a.m. when she heard him come through the front door. "You son of a..." she wailed from the top of the steps, throwing her glass down the stairs as her body fell down after it.

The surgery she underwent for her back injury made things worse. She complained of constant pain from the broken vertebrae, and the doctors just wrote her prescription after prescription. Anti-depressants came next. She developed severe OCD. Their 30,000 square foot home could never be clean enough for her. It looked like a staged palace to anyone who entered, everything shiny and in its place, Italian frescos adorning the walls, elegant furniture from France. He allowed her to buy anything she wanted. But she was never happy.

He couldn't remember now when he first became aware of his own unhappiness. At times, he did feel happy. When he closed on a particularly challenging deal, he felt like he could float through the roof; there was nothing he could not take on and conquer. Then there were the women…well, girls, mostly. They reminded him of his youth…or rather, a youth he felt he never had. They were the lucky ones, he thought. Unlike his eldest children, they were grateful for all he was giving them. That's all they wanted from him. His dick and his wallet. Sure, they were sometimes scared in the beginning, but he always managed to make them wet, so he knew they enjoyed it.

His wife didn't even want him anymore. He never showed interest in her body; he found it repulsive, and she knew it. Their relationship had become just another business arrangement.

"What is this event about again?" Derek asked.

"Human trafficking."

"Right." Derek could have cared less what it was about— they were all the same. But he would have to say a few words that night in front of the mayor. This was his time to play character three: the philanthropist.

"Yeah. You know a thing or two about it, don't you?" Margaret sneered.

He didn't feel he knew much about it at all. It wasn't like what he was doing with his girls in Bangkok, or on the Caribbean island he frequented as a party guest of fellow billionaires and world leaders; his girls wanted to work.

"You seem to know everything, Margaret, so why don't you tell me about it? Enlighten me."

What a hypocrite, Margaret thought to herself as she poured a stiff drink. "Do you want one?"

Derek shook his head. "I'm going to take a shower."

"Suit yourself."

Derek closed the bathroom door behind him. His wife had already gone back downstairs, but he wanted privacy. He'd undressed and was staring at himself in the mirror when a sharp pain shot out from his abdomen.

"What the?!" Derek began breathing heavy, leaning over onto the sink. He looked back into the mirror, and a repressed memory hit him as the pain got worse. The mirror. The medicine cabinet. Thomas. His son was only fourteen years old. He'd stolen his mother's prescription meds, along with God knows what else she kept in there, and invited his friends over. Derek had been in Thailand. Margaret was at their penthouse in New York, recovering from surgery.

One of the boys had taken too many drugs, fallen asleep outside, and was found in a lawn chair by the pool, dead from hypothermia. It could have been a very bad situation for Derek's image. He imagined the media frenzy that would have come from a subsequent legal battle, had he not paid off the officers who had arrived at the scene. They'd called him in Bangkok and he'd wired the money over immediately. "Death by accidental drowning," their report stated.

But seriously, the kid had been stupid, Derek thought. He was old enough to know what he was doing. Damn Thomas for inviting such an imbecile to the house! Thomas had taken some of the pills too, but he knew enough to not overdose. Thomas did introduce Monique to the drugs though, and Derek would never forgive him for that. He'd had to send the older kids through rehab before they even turned eighteen. Thank God, Katherine stayed clean.

"Damn you, Thomas! Damn you, Margaret!" Derek was screaming now in a hallucinatory frenzy as the memory pierced him.

"Dad, you should have been paying attention. You should have been there."

"Fuck you!"

"Yeah, Dad. Where the hell were you?!" Monique joined forces with Thomas now.

"Shut up! It's not my fault!" Derek tried to quell the voices, but it was no use. The pain had spread now, and he could no longer tell where it was coming from. The medicine cabinet. The pills. The dead kid by the pool.

Derek collapsed on the bathroom floor.

CHAPTER TWO

⋯⋯⟨∞⟩⋯⋯

THE CONTRACT

Derek came to the hospital, twenty-four hours later. He was high on morphine, but he'd already been told the news.

Pancreatic cancer.

Derek could not register what that meant; his experience felt ethereal. He lied in his hospital bed listening to the doctor's words, but they only floated in his head. He had no family members there to digest the words for him. He had no idea where anyone he knew was.

"Unfortunately, what you have is an aggressive form of cancer, Derek. The CT scan has revealed a tumor the size of a golf ball in your abdomen." The doctor had waited to see if Derek comprehended what he was saying. All Derek saw was a series of flying golf balls in his head, but he held the doctor's gaze, so the doctor continued.

"It's not surprising that it had not been caught earlier. There are not many noticeable symptoms early on, and many of the disease's more advanced symptoms—loss of appetite, abdominal pain, digestive problems, etc.—could easily be attributed to something much more minor."

The doctor paused again before asking, "Do you drink much, Mr. Stryker?"

Derek thought he understood this question. "Drink, yes. I could use a drink. A bourbon would be nice."

"Right." The doctor shifted his approach. "Get some rest, Mr. Stryker."

Rest. He did feel tired. Derek closed his eyes, but his dream state was interrupted as Margaret walked in the door with a nurse.

"Mrs. Stryker, I'm glad you're here. The patient is awake," the doctor nodded in Derek's direction.

"Oh, thank God!" Margaret had ridden to the hospital with him in the ambulance the day before, but the pressure of the situation had gotten to be too much for her. She had returned home for the night and gotten sloshed, trying to forget. She awoke shortly after 2 p.m. that day, finally sober enough to summon the household's driver to bring her back to the hospital.

She went straight to Derek's bedside and touched his face, "How do you feel? What is wrong?"

"Margaret, you're here. Where are the kids?"

"Thomas and Monique aren't answering my calls. You know how they are. And Katherine is in Africa, remember?"

"Africa? What the hell is she doing there?" Derek could barely muster the energy to scoff.

Margaret looked over at the doctor who interjected, "We just got the results back, Mrs. Stryker. Derek could use some rest, allow me to explain his circumstance."

"Margaret. Call me Margaret. What is going on? What's wrong with him?"

The doctor gently led Margaret to the corner of the room,

as the nurse checked Derek's vitals. "We are very sorry, but he has metastatic pancreatic cancer, Margaret. The scan revealed a large tumor in his pancreas and cancer that has spread to the liver and other areas of his abdomen. Unfortunately, there is little we can do for him at this stage."

"What do you mean, little you can do for him? We have money, doctor, that's not an issue. How much does it cost? We will wire it over right now."

"It's not an issue of money, Margaret. The cancer has spread so far that surgery and other procedures would be rendered futile. In fact, only about 20% of patients with pancreatic cancer are able to have surgery. His case is not uncommon."

"But you have drugs for this, don't you? I don't care if they have to be imported in from Mexico, tell us what drugs he needs and we will get them."

"I don't think you understand, Margaret. Aside from a dose of capecitabine, which can help with some of the disease's side effects, there is nothing that exists for the state of his condition. What you and the family really need to be considering at this point is where he would be most comfortable living out the last few months of his life."

These words, Margaret finally understood. She let out a wail that shook Derek in his bed, "What? What is it? Is the plane going down?" The nurse rearranged his pillows and tried to coax him back to rest, as the doctor led Margaret to the hallway.

"We have emotional support teams available, Margaret. I can have the nurse contact them on your behalf," the doctor began, but Margaret was already racing down the hallway, looking for the exit.

OVER THE NEXT COUPLE OF DAYS, DEREK BEGAN TO RECOVER his consciousness. He had a vague memory of having been visited by his wife a couple of days before, but he had heard nothing from her since. She must have managed to notify their children, however, because Thomas and Monique showed up at the hospital on his third day there.

He must admit he was happy to see them at first, but it soon became apparent what the motive for their visit was. Thomas began asking about his will, power of attorney, and estate plan documents. "We just want to make sure you don't have to worry yourself about it," Monique added.

Ha! I'm not dead yet, Derek thought. Thankfully, the nurse came in to notify his children that visiting hours were over, relieving him of the duty of having to answer their questions. He was also told by the nurse that Katherine had called to say she was on her way back from Africa.

He had told the nurse to tell her that it wouldn't be necessary—he wasn't that sick. He would be back at home and running his business shortly, he was sure. It couldn't be that serious; his business colleagues hadn't even contacted him. They must have heard what happened; after all, he hadn't shown up to the benefit a few nights before. They knew what he knew, he thought—it was just some abdominal pain. Nothing a few bourbons couldn't fix.

He couldn't wait to return home. The nurses kept looking at him with signs of pity; he kept asking for his mobile phone; he was sure he'd have a million voicemails that would need to be caught up on. They didn't give it to him, though. He must have left it at home. Instead, they just let him lie there, watching TV.

Late afternoon on his fourth day in the hospital, Derek

was semi-engrossed in a re-run episode of M*A*S*H when the nurse returned to the room to check his vitals. His condition had stabilized enough that his persistent request to be allowed to return home was finally granted.

"You are allowed to return home, for now, Derek, but have you given thought to what is going to be best for you in your situation?"

"What's best for me right now is to get the hell out of this petri dish."

"Fair enough. But, Derek…," the nurse felt inspired by Derek's forthright communication. "You know you're dying, right?"

"Yeah, yeah, that's what everyone's been trying to tell me, but look at me. I'm fine. I'm Derek Stryker. I'm one of the most powerful and richest men in the country. People like me don't die at fifty years of age."

The nurse did not give up, "You have terminal cancer, Derek. Terminal. No amount of money and power can change that. What you need to be focusing on are arrangements for these last few months of your life."

It was the way she looked at him. He had looked at others with those eyes when trying to explain a business deal—what don't you get? He used that look when he saw someone who was foolish. He would not be taken for a fool.

"Get me out of here," he would not process his grief in front of someone else.

His driver was called, and by 5 p.m. that evening he returned to an empty home, aside from his personal butler, Joseph. He had no idea where Margaret was, but he didn't care. He went to the room he felt most comfortable in—his home office. He locked the door behind him, offering him a bit of emotional security. He opened a bottle of bourbon he'd been saving for a "special occasion," with the intention of drinking the whole thing in one sitting. "Why not, I'm going to die soon anyway," he said out loud to himself. The significance of those words hit him like a two-by-four. I'm going to die. How can this be?! I'm a billionaire! Derek downed the first glass of bourbon in one straight shot down the throat. He then clasped his head in his hands and allowed himself to weep. Tears collected on a stack of papers before him; he looked down and tried to read the numbers on the spreadsheet, but they became blurred by his vision and the pooling wet stains on the paper.

What am I going to do with all this wealth? I didn't spend a lifetime making billions of dollars only to lose it all! Derek contemplated with a sense of desperation. He was well aware that his wife and children wanted nothing to do with Stryker Industries or any of the other businesses he'd developed. All they were interested in was liquidizing his assets in order to squander it. "Except Katherine," he said aloud. "Maybe I'll leave it all to her." He second-guessed himself, "Who am I kidding, she doesn't want anything to do with my businesses," he brushed the idea aside.

Derek pulled out the bottom left drawer of his mahogany, Kittinger partners desk and withdrew a box of Cohiba Cuban cigars. He lit one up, sat back in his brown leather executive chair, and remained in that position through the night and into the next morning.

IT WAS THE LIGHT THAT CAUSED DEREK TO STIR FROM HIS all-night frenzy. He became somewhat embarrassed at the recognition of drool down his chin and onto his shirt, but he brushed it off when he remembered the events of the past few days. *I only have a few months left to live.*

The solitude he craved the night before had passed, and he wanted nothing more than to be surrounded by love in that moment. It was a sad realization that he couldn't think of a single person who loved him that he could call. Katherine was on her way, true, but he had not heard anything from Thomas and Monique since their short visit the day before, and his wife had disappeared.

Derek could recall an enormous list of business colleagues whose numbers he could dial, but not a single friend. Wait, he suddenly remembered. Peter worked for Stryker Industries, but his relationship with Derek went beyond the business; they were both members of the Masonic order and had known each other since high school.

Both boys had been made fun of by their peers. They were the "geeks" at their all-boys prep school, and though Peter hadn't much liked Derek, Derek had come to his rescue their senior year in high school by convincing him to invest in his father's company. Derek felt a kinship in the short, awkward redhead. Like himself, he was picked on for being smart.

He gave Peter an initial sum of money, which Derek told him he'd be able to earn ten-fold within a year, at which time he could pay Derek back. Peter accepted and indeed made a very successful life for himself, managing the company's books and reaping rewards in equity.

Derek dialed Peter's number and anxiously waited for him to pick up. It felt like several minutes but was only a few rings before he heard Peter on the other line, "Hello? Derek?"

Derek struggled to find the words to explain to Peter why

he had called. His practiced business charisma failed to serve him in this situation.

"Peter, yes. It's Derek Stryker."

"I know, buddy. Hey, I heard you weren't feeling well or something? Everyone was wondering why you weren't at the benefit the other night."

"It's a bit more serious than that, Peter. I…I've been told I have pancreatic cancer."

The silence on the line pierced the air. Derek was acutely aware of the tick tock of the mantel clock across the room.

"Shit. Really? Are they sure?"

"Sure enough to tell me. They say I have six months, at best." Saying the words out loud to someone else made him wince. His voice cracked as he admitted, "I don't know what to do, Peter. What am I going to do with my businesses and estate? All these years of relentless work and achievements, down the drain…I don't know what to do…"

Only a few moments passed before Peter responded with assurance, "I'm coming over Derek. I have an idea. We're going to take a trip. Pack a nice suit."

Derek lacked a reason to argue. What else am I going to do, sit here and sulk? "Okay."

Peter hung up. Derek figured he had enough time to take a shower before he arrived. Upon entering the bedroom, he saw the disarray of the sheets. He couldn't remember the last time he'd seen the bed unmade; Margaret must have let the housekeeping staff off when she went wherever she went.

The cool water served him well. His hangover didn't feel quite so strong, and his mood shifted from despair to curiosity when he thought about what Peter had in mind. Derek dried off, shaved, and put on his nicest business suit.

Minutes later, he heard a car pull in the driveway. His butler must have recognized Peter and let him in because he soon heard Peter's voice.

"Derek! Where are you?"

"I'm up here. I'm coming," Derek made his way down the spiral staircase. He carried his briefcase, but no luggage. He didn't expect to be gone long.

Upon seeing Derek, Peter noted how different he looked. His face had become sullen; he was amazed at how quickly jaundice had crept in. He looked nothing at all like the man he'd seen just a few weeks ago, and even further from the boy he remembered from high school.

"Come, my driver is waiting." The two didn't speak as they made their way to the airport. Peter had already called Derek's pilot, who'd begun prepping the plane for a flight to Los Angeles. Few words were spoken in flight, either. Peter told Derek he preferred that the people they were going to see explain what the visit was about.

Derek passed the six-and-a-half-hour flight looking out the window. Suddenly, being so high in the clouds took on new meaning for him. When they landed in L.A., a limo and driver were already waiting for them; Peter had arranged everything.

The two were driven forty-five minutes into the hills in the outskirts of Los Angeles. It was easy to lose track of where they'd driven, but Derek suspected that was intentional. He gazed at the decadent mansions scattered on the hillside until finally they were driven through a forested stretch of land where the road ended at a driveway.

There was an elaborate iron gate outside the property, through which Derek gauged Peter had been many times.

Peter leaned outside the car window and punched a code into the box by the gate, and immediately it opened up before them. They continued to ride up the expansive driveway, and even someone as accustomed to luxury as Derek couldn't help but be in awe of the property.

Sculptures stood amid gardens of impeccably landscaped trees and plants, with flowers bursting in a breathtaking rainbow of color. Manmade cascades flowed over carefully designed rock formations. Derek realized the ponds on the property must consist of saltwater, as there were tide pools within them; he could see starfish and anemone. It looked the closest to paradise Derek could have imagined.

At the roundabout before the grand entrance to a magnificent, classic yet contemporary mansion, arose a round, palatial fountain. Standing around the fountain were three men, dressed exquisitely in business suits and wearing welcoming faces. As Peter and Derek made their way out of the limo, a tall, older gentleman came forward to shake Derek's hand, "Welcome, Derek. We've heard so much about you. It's a pleasure to finally meet you." The other two men nodded in agreement. Derek's curiosity gave way to confusion; he looked toward Peter for an explanation, but Peter just smiled, shrugged his shoulders, and mouthed, "Trust me."

The men guided Peter and Derek into the mansion, through a grand hallway, and into a spectacular library. Marble floors, vaulted ceilings decorated with Spanish fresco paintings, and handcrafted wood shelves laid claim to thousands of antique volumes of books. Derek looked around the room in awe, as he was offered tea in a set of the most beautiful Flora Danica Tea Set and told to make himself comfortable around the mahogany conference table. Derek accepted the tea but his patience was growing thin, "Alright, gentlemen. What is all this about? What do you know about me?"

The man who had first greeted Derek took the floor, "Yes, we were told you like to get down to business, and so we will. We are part of a secret society, Derek. Only the extraordinary elite are aware of our existence, but our general members number in the thousands. Peter has spoken of you as a possible recruit for the past several years, but only now has the urgency of the matter been brought to our attention. We are aware that you're dying, Derek."

Those words hadn't gotten any easier for Derek to hear.

"But you need not worry," the man continued. We have an offer for you that we trust you will not want to refuse. It is a privilege to be on the receiving end of what we are about to offer you, Derek. We are in agreement that you merit a high position within our society."

"What society is this?"

"It's called Gemini." Derek had never heard of it.

"Remember, not everyone gets invited into the society, especially of the level at which this invitation extends. You must recognize that it is an honor that you have been chosen."

He was intrigued. A little flattery had always gone a long way with Derek. "What is your offer?"

"Peter here has told us of your predicament. You have worked very hard to be where you are today; you learned to use your brilliant mind to generate great wealth in this lifetime. Now, you are unsure about what to do with it. It would be a pity to lose it all upon your death, wouldn't it?"

It was a hypothetical question, but it deliberately gave time for Derek to reimagine the consequence.

"The good news is, thanks to your friend Peter, you won't

have to. He has brought you to our attention, and we want to include you in our prestigious society. Congratulations, Derek."

Derek smiled, oblivious as to how the charismatic technique he'd used in so many business meetings was now being used upon him.

The gentleman continued, "Now, let me explain how this works. Induction into the society requires an understanding that upon your death, you do not simply die, but you are reborn. I know you have not given much thought to this in the past, but it is a truth you will soon come to experience for yourself."

Derek looked to Peter, who nodded in agreement. He bought into this? - he thought with sudden skepticism.

"How come I have never heard of this before?" Derek questioned.

"This information is not shared widely among the public. However, if you spoke to a number of elite business professionals and celebrities, you would find that this knowledge is widely accepted as truth, among those who are eligible. Allow me to show you something," the man pushed a button on the wall, hidden behind a book. Instantly, the bookshelf rotated, revealing an opening to a long hallway.

Lining the hallway were wooden file cabinets, organized alphabetically. "Go ahead. Take a look," the man motioned for Derek to open any particular drawer. He opened the one nearest to him labeled "At," and removed a leather-bound file folder.

"These folders include the contracts of members past and present who have joined our elite society."

Derek thumbed through the folder, shocked to recognize

the signatures of such high- profile individuals. Some of them had already passed away—he knew them as colleagues of his father. Many were still living and were people he had done business with or had drunk with at lavish parties. He couldn't help but feel like he had been left out again—just like in high school.

"Do you wish to know who some of those who passed away became in their next lives?"

Derek nodded.

"John Atkins, for example, is now known to the world as Caleb Munson. Matthew Atkinson is George Taylor. Very wealthy men, Derek."

The names were familiar to Derek, the former an award-winning young actor, and the latter a championship NFL quarterback for the Dallas Cowboys.

"By joining the society, you will be like these men, Derek. You will return in the next life a very wealthy man, just as you are in this life."

"How does this work? What do you need from me?"

"Let's return to the conference room." The man led Derek back to the table, where the other men were still sitting. The man withdrew several sheets of paper from a portfolio on the table and a golden pen from his shirt pocket. "This contract officially inducts you into Gemini. It is signed simultaneously with the release of the necessary funds and assets, which will be placed in our vaults for safekeeping until your next life."

"How much do I have to pay to join?"

"Well, Derek, don't look at it in terms of payment. It's really an investment. You're a businessman, so I know you know the difference. The money you invest now will be given back to you in your next life. If you don't sign the contract, when you die, you will have lost all that you've worked so hard to achieve. We are offering you the opportunity to take it with you, Derek."

Derek liked the sound of that.

"Naturally, you'd like to leave some money to your wife and children. The society allows a generous allotment of 10% of your wealth to be left to provide for the care of your family."

Derek pondered the transaction. That would leave four billion dollars for his family.

"Would you like to sign the contract now, Derek? We have a deed of trust already written up."

A shooting pain in Derek's abdomen made him double over before he regained the ability to speak. Since the hospital, up until that moment, he had merely felt light digestive discomfort. The pain served as a timely reminder of just how little life he had left in this body.

The man caught a glimpse of hesitation in Derek's eyes. He looked at him compassionately and reminded him, "You don't want to wait too long to make this decision."

Derek looked again at Peter. "Remember, Derek, how you helped me to invest in your father's company? I owe you a great deal, and this is my way to repay you."

I trust you, Derek thought.

"Yes. Give me the contract." Derek was handed the golden pen and a clipboard, upon which another man had placed the contract. He thought of all the files of names he had just seen, of people far more famous and influential than he. As he penned his familiar scrawl across the bottom of each page, he felt like he was taking advantage of the business deal of a lifetime.

After the last page, he handed the clipboard back to the

leader, who in turn dropped red-hot wax onto the document and stamped it with a symbol that Derek recognized as the Star of David.

"Derek, may I be the first to officially welcome you to Gemini. The symbol on this document ensures that the universe will protect you and your wealth from all six directions—north, south, east, west, up, and down." All four of the men before him took turns shaking his hand and patting him on the back. He felt part of something bigger—more secure and more loved than he had ever felt in his life.

"I always knew you were a smart man, Derek," Peter grinned. "You're making an excellent choice."

DEREK RETURNED TO HIS HOME IN CONNECTICUT straight away after the meeting. He felt confident in his decision, but physically and emotionally exhausted. The abdominal pain had only gotten worse. He could barely hold down solid food. And then there were the hiccups; he kept developing bouts of hiccups that shot pain throughout his body so intense that at times he wished he would just die. The drugs the hospital had given him did practically nothing.

His daughter Katherine arrived at the house the day after his return from Los Angeles. She had relentlessly doted on him, bringing him food he would not eat, but trying her best to keep him comfortable. He was happy to not be alone, but he hated to have his daughter see him like this.

Margaret was completely absent; Katherine had informed him she had gone to New York to stay in their penthouse. She had told her she couldn't handle "being at home right now." She had actually asked Katherine to "call her after he's dead"—words that stung Katherine's heart to hear, and that she wouldn't dream of telling her father.

Thomas and Monique had come to visit him one more time at the house. They insisted on gaining access to his estate documents, and that is when he shared the news.

"Everything has already been taken care of," he told them. "The house and cars will be left to Margaret, and $4 billion of my estate will be evenly divided among you three children and Margaret."

"Four billion?!" Thomas had exclaimed. "What about the rest?"

"You need not worry about the rest. It is in good hands." Derek caught a hint of a smile on Katherine's lips. He had been right; she didn't much care about the money. Like himself, she likely felt justice in her siblings' disappointment. That was the last time Derek would see his two eldest children; they parted in frustration, slamming the door on their way out. Katherine stayed behind and didn't bring the topic up again.

It would only be nine weeks before Derek's body would begin to severely shut down. His daily care had become too much for his daughter, even with the assistance of his butler, Joseph, and he finally agreed to be brought into hospice. To him, the move signified the end of this life. Part of him rested comfortably in knowing that a new, richly abundant life would succeed him, but nonetheless, the dying process was much more challenging than he had imagined. It was Katherine that was making it so difficult.

"Daddy, hang in there! You can do this, you're a strong man! I need you, Daddy!"

Derek had never truly felt needed before—not emotionally. Plenty of people "needed" his money. There had been many women who needed his body. But here before him was a beautiful woman whom he had given life to, who was saying that she needed him in order to continue living herself. He fought for his life, simply for that reason. But eventually, he was ready to accept his fate. He knew it was time. I want this to end.

Derek yearned for a moment without his daughter in the room. It was too hard for him to let go with her there. He fought with all of his power to hide the pain and pretend he was sleeping. After fifteen minutes of feigned calm, Katherine finally excused herself to use the restroom. She squeezed his hand and whispered, "I'll be right back, Daddy." He waited until he heard the door quietly close behind her, leaving only the nurses in the room.

"Aghhhhhhhh," Derek allowed himself to thrash violently in bed as the nurses tied him down and increased the doses of morphine that were being injected into his system through tubes.

Tubes were everywhere. His vision became so cloudy that he closed his eyes to avoid getting dizzy, but images of tubes remained in his mind. He was inside one now…swimming through the tube in a pool of morphine, trying to stop himself from going through the dark tunnel he saw at the end. Suddenly, he was very afraid to die.

"No!!!" was the last word that echoed throughout the room before Derek Stryker's heart beat for the last time.

CHAPTER THREE

THE REGRET

The tunnel wasn't as dark as it had appeared when alive. In fact, it was illuminated now with a bright light that made it appear less frightening. But Derek was moving so fast through it…it felt as though he was traveling as fast as the speed of light itself.

The further he was propelled, the lighter his body felt. In fact, he wasn't particularly aware of his body at all. It was as though the intense pain he had suffered just a moment before had evaporated and risen into the atmosphere as gravity ceased to exist.

He had no idea where he was going, but he didn't have to wait long to get there. With a blinding flash, Derek emerged through the other end of the tunnel and instantly felt what in human terms would be described as ecstasy—a blissful state of pure love. Derek didn't recall ever having felt this sensation while in his body.

He understood he was out of his body now, as he could see himself; he was observing himself from an elevated position. He could see not just Derek the body and personality but understand who he was—who he was and had been, since the beginning of time. He was amazed to discover how vast his being was—that he wasn't a body or mind at all, but rather an effervescent soul—something Derek the man wasn't sure existed.

Though he had no idea where he was in time and space, he felt at peace. All he saw before him was crystalline light. A sound that could be likened to a reverberating "om" could be heard throughout the space; he found it soothing. He knew he was safe.

He recognized, in fact, that he was not alone. There was a being in the distance, in human form. He no sooner placed his attention on the man than his consciousness took him there, as if in flight. He now stood before this majestic figure. It was a man that appeared to be over seven feet tall with dark, wavy long hair and all-knowing eyes. He was stunning; beautiful, even.

"Hello, Derek. I am Michael, your guide." The words weren't spoken, but rather telepathically communicated.

"No, this isn't heaven." The man "spoke" again; he had read Derek's thoughts. "This is where all souls come to be processed and to prepare for their next incarnation."

"No, I am not God, either. As I said, I am your guide. I have taken a human form because that is what your consciousness currently recognizes. In reality, all I am is energy—same as you."

The voice vibrated in Derek's head. He felt overwhelmed, trying to process what he was hearing and experiencing. He fell into what seemed like a deep sleep, but he maintained consciousness. He remained floating, as he felt every cell of his body begin to heal. His already weightless state became even lighter as he felt an invigorating energy course through him.

The colors around him became brighter; his senses were deeply awakened. There were mountains and streams clear as crystal. Everything around him moved like liquid; the joy he felt was childlike and pure. He wanted nothing more than to remain there, floating among the fields of flowers and abundant wildlife—he could see deer, wolves, bears, salmon…all peacefully cohabitating. Every being understood its place in the interconnectedness of all things.

"I'm going to offer you a great blessing now, Derek." Michael appeared and jolted Derek out of his deep state of awareness. "We call it a life review. This is the opportunity to re-live the most pivotal moments in your most recent life. Are you ready?"

He didn't know what he agreed to, but Derek's thoughts replied, "Yes, I think so." Instantly, he began watching what seemed like a movie of his life, starting in 1941 at the moment of his birth. But he didn't just see what happened in his life, he felt every minute's emotion associated with the experience—and not just his emotions, but the emotions of all of those around him.

He was now a year old, screaming for his mother's breast and desperate to nurse. His mother did not even make eye contact with him; she passed him off to the nanny and slammed the door behind her. It was the first of many visions where he yearned for his mother and felt the intense pain of separation, fear, and frustration. Where was she? Would she ever come back?

In another vision, he was five years old. Young Derek was playing with his football in his father's office when he broke a rare statue his father had received as a gift from a business colleague in Thailand. Derek couldn't remember now if he'd broken it on purpose—he often fought for attention from his parents—or if it was an accident. Either way, he could feel both the emotional and physical pain as his father hit him in punishment. He was never allowed in his father's office again after that.

Now he was nine years old, and he'd fallen sick with pneumonia. His parents had booked a business trip to Thailand which they insisted on keeping, even though he had a temperature of 104 degrees. He could feel the heat now while watching his younger self; he began to sweat, and chills ran through his body just as they had back then. He had wanted nothing more than the comfort of having them home with him—to know and to feel that they cared. He could feel that familiar sense of abandonment and anger. Where were they??

His anger only progressed throughout his life. However, he managed to find various outlets for his frustration. Sullenly, he watched as he developed into the father figure that he had loved and hated simultaneously. Derek was not there for his children. He considered them distractions from work—which was the one thing he had learned from his father how to do well.

He watched as his first child was born and subsequently died in her sleep two months later. He felt practically no emotion at the time—or rather, he did, but he ignored it and denied it to the point that he forgot he'd ever felt anything. Now, however, he could see and feel his wife's pain. How could he have been so blind when he was alive? He had entered his wife's body now; the sharp, stabbing pain in her heart was so extreme, she wished she had died along with their child.

He could read her thoughts; This is my fault. I'm a terrible mother. How could I have let this happen?! I don't deserve to live! Margaret turned to Derek then, looking for comfort, but his back was turned to her. She cried harder as Derek spoke, "I need to get some air. I'm going to take a walk." And with that, he left her alone. He got drunk and didn't return until several hours later—after the paramedics had already arrived and taken the baby with them.

His wife slipped into drugs, as he dove into sex. It was several months before his wife would sleep with him again... what was he supposed to do? He had thought. He had affairs with countless women—just as he had seen his father do. There had to be some form of relief in it, right? He remembered thinking. He kept searching for it but never truly found it. Now he could see how fruitless that effort had been—and how much it had hurt Margaret.

And his kids... the oldest two, Thomas and Monique... they knew so much more than he thought they knew. And they felt so much more; his absence had been severely painful for them. How did he not know that? It suddenly made so much sense that they'd entered a world of escapism as well.

He watched as his son looked for him in the stands of every Little League game he ever played. He has to come, Thomas thought. He promised he would. Over the years, his son's hope turned to anger, and then to hate. Thomas broke into Margaret's medicine cabinet as a teenager, as a last resort—he decided it was drugs or suicide, and he figured he'd try the first before he tried the latter.

Growing up, Monique was perhaps even more ignored than Thomas had been, since Derek had only immersed himself more and more into the business as he got older. Derek could see her now—she was five years old and was bringing him a drawing. It was a picture of the family. Each member was standing with their arms around each other, and a heart was drawn above them. "Is this some kind of joke?" he'd asked her. He felt like his five-year-old daughter was mocking him. He certainly didn't feel the love in the family. He could feel now how she had merely drawn what she'd wanted her family to be like. It was a silent cry for help.

Derek watched as Thomas found temporary relief from the pain through drugs and, therefore, introduced Monique to his discovery. Thomas couldn't bear to see Monique suffer like he did when he was sober. Life for the two children had no meaning. It was devoid of love, ripe with dysfunction, and the material gifts they received from their parents were an insulting remittance for the only thing they'd ever wanted from them all along. They didn't know what love felt like. Derek felt it now—a hollow emptiness that was beyond the level of void he had felt in his own life.

Derek watched his life fall aimlessly and irreversibly into a pattern of sexual addiction by the time Katherine was born. He loved Katherine from the start, in a way he had not felt for his older children. How deeply drawn to her beauty he had been. She garnered more attention from him than his other children, and certainly more than what he gave his wife. It was hard for him to take his eyes off of her. He was charmed by her innocence, by her intelligence, by her boldness.

He was attracted to her, no doubt, but he denied to himself that it was ever in a sexual way. She was his daughter, for Christ's sake. Instead, he found alternate ways to express the guilt behind what he felt when he looked at his youngest daughter.

Katherine was a blossoming twelve-year-old girl when he

began experimenting with young girls. He did to their bodies what he withheld doing from Katherine's. He told himself they liked it. Now, watching the replay of girl after girl who he had been with, he could feel what they had felt. He felt their desperation, their disgust—while he got high on domination.

Disgust. That was the emotion he felt now, watching himself in a replay. But also pity—for the boy, he had been. The boy who felt the same sense of abandonment as his two oldest children.

His heart had become so hardened by the time he entered his forties…harder still as he reached fifty. It was because of that resoluteness that he was able to lead Stryker Industries from a twenty-billion-dollar business to forty billion. He was wondering now why those numbers had mattered so much to him?

His life review moved now to two men who had been affected by his business decisions. One was Jon Baumgartner. He had liked the guy; he was a fun poker mate and a good man, but he didn't have good business sense. Derek had loaned him $850 million to develop a casino in upstate New York in 2006.

Another colleague he lent a significant amount of money to was Matthew Strausser; he saw him now, toasting champagne to the opening of his new hotel on Hilton Head Island. Neither man had read the contract terms sufficiently well; they had trusted him as a friend. When the 2008 recession hit, Jon and Matthew—among many others he had lent money to—could not make payments. They defaulted on their loans and Derek acquired both the casino and the hotel, now added to his giant portfolio of investments.

These two men took the hit particularly hard. During

his life, Derek never learned of what happened to them after they'd signed away their assets. Of course, if he had, he would have brushed the occurrences off anyway.

Now, he watched as each man sat in anguish. Jon was in his Manhattan office, on the twenty-fourth floor with giant windows overlooking the bustling city below. He sat in his plush leather desk chair, gazing at the cars that drove by in an endless chain of duty.

Everyone seemed to have a purpose—places to be, people to meet, deals to be done. Jon did not feel part of that world anymore; his life was over, as far as he was concerned. No one would do business with a failed man such as himself. Derek felt what Jon felt in those last moments—utter and complete hopelessness.

Jon reached into his briefcase for the shotgun he previously kept at home for safety. He didn't need to contemplate the action; he'd already decided to do it the night before, and he wanted to do it here—at the office, he acquired at the height of his career. The gun was already loaded; he raised it to his head as he stared out across the city at the bank that had previously held his money. "Here's to having had the courage to try," he spoke out loud before pulling the trigger.

"Wait!! It's okay; I'll forgive you the money!" Derek forgot for a moment he was already dead—that it was too late, that Jon couldn't hear him and he too, was already dead. Derek was crying now, what a fool he had been! All he'd seen was the bottom line; he never saw the people, never imagined the pain.

He didn't have to imagine anything now—it was all made real for him. The review moved on to Matthew. "No, not again…" Derek panicked as he saw Matthew making a rope knot in his penthouse apartment. They had, in fact, made the deal in that very room—beneath the extravagant chandelier that hung in Matthew's dining room.

Matthew had positioned a chair beneath the chandelier and was hanging the rope from it. Matthew's wife had taken their nine-year-old daughter out shopping just fifteen minutes before—he hadn't yet told them that the family was about to lose everything. He couldn't bring himself to do it. This way, he wouldn't have to.

He stood on the chair and placed the noose around his neck. He then kicked the chair away and let himself hang. He'd been there three minutes when he heard his wife getting the keys to the door, "Honey, go tell Daddy I forgot his credit card." He was gasping for his last breath when the door opened and his eyes trained on his daughter's, "Daddy, nooooo!!!!" Matthew instantly felt regret, but it was too late.

It was too much for Derek. He could feel not only Matthew's suffering—his body fighting for air, his emotional agony and remorse at what he was doing to his family—but now he could feel the trauma Matthew's daughter was going through—the confusion, the shock, the grief; her life would be forever scarred by this experience.

"ENOUGH!" Derek cried out, "Get me away from here! STOP!!!" Michael instantly adhered to Derek's request.

"You see, Derek, nothing anyone does in life goes unnoticed by the higher realm—and nothing exists in a vacuum. Everything we do, say, and think has repercussions on everyone around us—even strangers."

"I just wanted love," Derek was crying now. "I thought I wanted money, but what I really wanted was love."

"That's right, Derek."

"I felt nothing when I was alive. All of these emotions I just went through…where were they then?"

"You blocked them out, Derek. With alcohol, with sex. With your quest for money. You did not die of cancer, Derek. You died of an accumulation of toxic energy—energy that developed from your lack of ability to process emotion. Humans like to blame outside forces for the state of their health, but in truth, their worst enemy is their nervous system. The tension inside you is what translates itself into symptoms of disease. You held a lot of tension, Derek—and not just from this life, but from many, many lives before."

"What other lives?"

"You have lived hundreds of lives. We can't go through them all now. You may have had different names and different bodies, but you have almost always made the same choices. At times, you have chosen to deal with your emotions, but you have never sought to master them. Without doing the work—whether it be through meditation, journaling, counseling, energy healing, or any other of the many methods available to humankind—those pains and shadows will be carried with you into the afterlife and will continue to haunt your next incarnation."

"My next incarnation?"

"Yes, Derek, you have more lives ahead of you. And you will have the opportunity to choose differently."

"If what you're saying is true, can I choose who I will be in my next life?"

"Yes, you may. You may choose the name and body you will reincarnate into, as well as your parents."

"I know who I want to be! Make me poor, Michael! Make me a beggar in…Calcutta! I no longer want to be rich. Money has caused so many people pain; I am done with that Michael. Make me a poor man!"

"I wish I could grant you that request, Derek, but I cannot."

"What do you mean, you said I could choose who I will be!"

"You can, for the most part. But remember, Derek," Michael looked into Derek's eyes with regret, "You signed a sacred contract."

"Contract? What are you talking about?"

"You joined Gemini, Derek. You committed to returning in your next life with the wealth you left behind in the last."

"Wait, you're telling me that was real? I mean, I know I believed that when I was alive, but now…You've shown me the bigger picture, Michael. I've seen how corrupt money is. Gemini had to have been just another scheme—not unlike the business deals I used to conduct—simply to take advantage of others. That can't be real, Michael. Tell me that wasn't real!"

"It was as real as anything, Derek. One of your great writers, George Orwell, said it best: 'Reality exists in the human mind, and nowhere else.' That contract was constructed in the human mind, and therefore will play out in future human forms."

Derek couldn't believe what he was hearing. "No! There has to be a way to void that contract!"

"I am afraid not. But that's not necessarily a bad thing. You have a grand opportunity before you in your next life, if you only choose to take advantage of it. It's an opportunity you have passed by in many previous lives."

"What is it?"

"First, you have to acknowledge the existence of the

soul—your own, and that of all other beings. Despite humanity's technological advances, the human condition has not changed. Humans tend to neglect the soul, choosing instead to focus on the mind and the body. This neglect has caused an exorbitant amount of unnecessary pain on earth. For only by looking deeply inward to the soul can a person discover the key to coping with life's problems."

"Okay, so humans have a soul. I acknowledge that. So, what?"

"It's not enough to acknowledge the soul in the afterlife—everyone becomes aware of the soul after death. You have to choose to remember what you understand now, while in human form. This requires a journey deep inside oneself, to in fact discover your true self. This effort of self-discovery may be painful, but it is essential to overcome the pains and afflictions of your past and transcend into the next state—for yourself, and for the planet."

"What next state?"

"One that is built on a foundation of love and compassion—love for ourselves, love for all other beings, and love for the planet on which you live. What is important to know is that to reach that state of peace, the participation of only 3.5% of earth's population is required.

"Seems remarkably low, doesn't it? The human race is well below that level of participation. What your planet needs is a great leader, someone with the ability to influence the masses. Since on your planet, those with the most wealth have the most influence; such a shift will require a redistribution of wealth away from those who use money to further advance their condition and toward those who use their wealth for the advancement of society as a whole.

"So, you see, wealth by itself is not evil, Derek. This is why you have a great opportunity before you in your next life. But there is something you must do first."

"What is that?"

"You must understand here, in the afterlife, what led you to who you were in this past life. You will carry this knowledge with you into the next life—although you may not remember, at first, what you already know. But if you choose to seek a higher purpose, you will come to experience a great wave of understanding when this knowledge is presented to you. You will know in your soul that it is truth."

"I think I understand. I could see the patterns play out in my life review. I re-enacted the patterns of my parents. I was not there for my children, nor for my wife. And I suppressed my emotions, choosing instead to focus on work and the accumulation of wealth."

"Good, Derek. That is very good. Continue."

"I...I could see that I never really had a personal identity. When I was young, I played the role of who I thought my parents wanted me to be. I felt how my mother wanted love so badly from my father that she resented me for the love I needed from her. So, my experience as a child was a result of my parents' experiences before me, wasn't it? It wasn't my fault, after all, was it?"

"Of course, it wasn't your fault, Derek. It wasn't your parents' fault either, though. I could show you their parents before them, but I believe you get the point. It's not a matter of blame. What is important to understand is that everyone always has the choice to choose differently—differently than our parents before us, and differently than we have chosen before ourselves.

"These choices are not easy. It is not only our backgrounds and those of our caretakers that influence individuals, but it is society as a whole. The society humans have created is not one that allows children to grow into who they really are. Your society conditions children according to the requirements of a consumer culture."

"How does it do that?"

"It implants doubt in children's minds about who they are—about what they need to be happy. It preaches a disconnect between the human mind, body, and soul. Your religions often even teach that, if you do have a soul, it is damned due to having committed 'sins'—and, interestingly, those sins can be forgiven if you pay money."

"That's true. Everything seems to be about money, isn't it?"

"Yes and no. Money isn't real, you know. Humans have given it a value based on what can be bought with it—but in essence, it is merely a tool to direct towards that which is most valued in the human mind and soul. What do you think all humans truly desire, Derek?"

"Love. Happiness. Health. Peace."

"Exactly. So, can you imagine what would happen if all efforts on your planet were re-directed with those goals in mind for everyone?"

"I must admit, those goals seem somewhat impossible."

"They're not impossible. I promise you that. People on your planet are already taking action to create that world. You will see. But they need the support of many more humans in alignment with those goals."

Derek let out a quiet sigh.

"Are your ready, Derek?"

"Ready for what?"

"To choose who you will be in your next life."

"Well, I guess so. So, I have to be wealthy, right?"

"Yes. You will have to take actions to regain your wealth again, but if you put in the effort, it will come back to you."

"Okay. So…I want the experience of having parents who truly want me and love me deeply."

"No problem."

"And I don't want to be raised in a big city…especially not New York or L.A. Those cities are so full of corruption. How about a rural town in…Oregon?"

"You got it."

"I want to be a male again. And attractive."

"Are you sure about that? Understand that you'll still face the same temptations you've faced in previous lives," Michael gave Derek an all-knowing look, but his lips curled up into a smile to reveal that even celestial beings have a sense of humor.

"Yes, I can handle it. But…"

"Yes?"

"What if I stray from my path? How can I get back on?"

"Remember, you won't be alone on this journey, Derek. As your guide, I will always be with you to send you reminders of who you really are, though you may not be aware of my presence at all times."

"What if I miss your reminders? I mean, I can be pretty dense."

"I understand your concern. As a human, you will have free will, and there is always the chance you will make choices that are not in your highest interest. However, we can agree now that if on your twenty-fifth birthday if you are not on the path to become awakened—if you have not recognized that love is the greatest power—I will make myself known to you. We will undergo a spiritual journey together."

"Okay. Deal."

"Alright, Derek. And what will your new name be then?"

"Eli," Derek didn't hesitate. It was the first name of his math teacher in middle school, who had been the only one to acknowledge his skill with numbers.

"Eli, it is. Are you ready to be re-born? You will start at conception."

"You mean I have to go through the whole process of being a...fetus?"

Michael laughed, "Yes, of course. Who a human becomes is influenced by factors he or she experiences well before taking bodily form. You should know that by now."

"Alright. So be it. Let's do this."

"Very well. Now close your eyes..."

CHAPTER FOUR

ELI, THE BOY

I t was a warm, spring day in 1992 when Carol and Robert brought their son into the world. Nearly everything went as planned. It was their first child, and they had been cautioned by many members of their community that a natural home birth would be risky. At twenty-eight years old, however, Carol was in great health; she was petite, but she claimed her German descent made her hardy.

She and her husband had been trying to get pregnant for the past three years. She'd known even the night they'd made love that this was the time their dreams would come true. She felt a calm reassurance that the pregnancy and delivery would be smooth.

Her husband Robert felt the same, although his protective nature made him more cautious than Carol. He had suggested that perhaps they should spend her last trimester at her parents' home just outside of Coeur d'Alene, Idaho. There was a highly-rated medical facility there, just in case, and her mother would be there to help with the newborn. She would be able to get more rest that way, he added. But Carol insisted on staying home and giving birth at their farm outside of Brownsville, Oregon. She had envisioned it that way.

"Besides," Carol explained, "The hospital in Brownsville is only fifteen minutes away. And no doubt when I go into labor, Mom and Dad will already be on their way here to welcome their grandson to the world." Her parents were even more thrilled at the prospect of a new family member than Carol and Robert, if that were possible. Carol was an only child, so this grandchild was extra special. Carol reminded her husband that their midwife, Susie, had delivered over one hundred babies, and she would be there by their side through it all.

It was important to Carol to have the baby at home. Robert and Carol would never have been able to afford this gem of a property had it not been gifted to them upon the passing of Carol's aunt. Her Aunt Maggie and Uncle Mike had no children and thus no heirs; Mike had passed four years before Maggie due to a stroke. Maggie had continued to live on the farm until her death, despite the advice of her family members to move into a senior home. However, the property had not been maintained for quite some time.

Carol recalled how her aunt had always been described as "the rebel" in the family. She ran away from home at the age of sixteen, determined to join the demonstrations in San Francisco against the Vietnam War. She'd always felt like the black sheep of the family; her parents had raised her with love, but they just couldn't understand her more progressive ideals. Her family had a small-town mindset that to Maggie seemed simple and blind to what global conditions currently called for.

When Maggie met Mike two years later at a political rally in Eugene, Oregon, she felt understood. Mike was seven years older than she was, but at eighteen years old, Maggie was old enough to get married. They bought the Brownsville property at a price Mike's employment with a lobbying firm in Eugene could afford; they had somewhat resolved that their hippie lifestyle would be better lived in the country. They had tried desperately to have children but to no avail. Their commitment to each other, however, was profound; they loved the little life they created for themselves on the farm and satisfied their desire to nurture by lovingly taking care of their goats, cows, dogs, cats, and any injured animal they found.

Maggie never completed her education, but she was known around central Oregon for her innate ability for healing. She had formed friendships with Native American women from the nearby Kalapuya tribe, who taught her various medicinal treatments. Carol credited her passion for plants and animals to her aunt, who had promised to teach her "everything she knew."

Carol fondly recalled her visits to Aunt Maggie and Uncle Mike's farm with her parents each summer. Maggie and her older sister Jane, Carol's mother, had a close relationship. Though Maggie still didn't feel like her parents understood her, she had resolved to forgo any ill-thoughts or effort to try to change her parents and focus instead on the healthy and loving upbringing they had offered her.

Jane had, in fact, been the catalyst for helping Maggie heal her relationship with their parents, by encouraging Maggie to invite the whole family to the farm. Their parents couldn't have been prouder that the hard-working ideals they had hoped to instill in their daughter were being demonstrated by the beauty of Maggie and Mike's property.

When Robert and Carol assumed ownership of the property, they could see how well-loved it had once been. Built in the 1940s, the home retained a lot of its character and charm. The home had what Carol called "soul." She fell in love with its gingerbread trim, and her favorite room was the kitchen, with its breakfast nook and walk-in pantry. She could picture cooking fresh and healthy meals for her family in the home.

The sitting room had inviting window seats that beckoned a good book, as did the wrap around porch from which one's eyes could gaze upon the 400 acres of national forest that ran up against their thirty-acre property, and their ears would take in the babbling creek that ran nearby. Across the way, a hay barn, milking shed, and orchard that included fig, apple, and peach trees, along with a hundred-year-old English walnut tree, completed the picture.

But it wasn't perfect. It took Robert and Carol seven years to save up enough money to bring the farm back to where it once was. They replaced the leaky roof, missing panels of the old barn, and Robert built a door for the shed. The exterior of the house had been painted bright white with red trim, the carpets had been ripped up and the original hardwood floors restored. The land itself had needed massive work; it was significantly overgrown with blackberries, which were quite the undertaking to clear.

In the past three years, however, the two had been able to enjoy the fruits of their labor and were ready to welcome a child into their beloved home.

Carol opted for a water birth; they had made the third bedroom in their 2,000 square foot farmhouse into a nursery, and it would serve as the delivery room. Plants adorned the walls—succulents and air plants hung in little planter boxes, and a giant Pothos plant hung by the window, its long stems stretched in every which direction across the ceiling. She wanted her child to be able to wake up, look up, and feel like he was in the forest.

Susie, the midwife, had the bath water in the inflatable tub warmed to just under ninety-eight degrees at the time Carol went into labor. She had made a tincture of cramp bark and chamomile, which she gave to Carol to help ease labor pains. After four hours of labor, their child entered the world. He was the perfect mix of both parents—his hair was light, almost blonde like his mother's, and he had his father's olive skin and hazel eyes. The baby's name had not been in question; it had come to Carol in a dream shortly after conception. He would be named Eli—the Greek word for "high" or "ascended."

Carol's parents arrived to greet their new grandson shortly after the delivery. They had driven as fast as they could from Haycrop, Idaho. Jane took one look at the boy, cradled up against his mother's chest, and knew he was going to bring the family great pride and joy. She remained at Carol's for the next three months, helping prepare meals and do laundry so that Carol could rest between the baby's frequent feedings. Robert was, therefore, able to focus on the farm chores. Carol's dad helped Robert with the animals for the first week of the baby's life but then had to return to maintain their property back in Idaho.

It gave Carol great pleasure to be able to raise the boy on their farm. Together with her husband, they wanted their baby to grow up the way they had, in the small town where they'd met in high school—living connected to nature and learning the value of hard work on the farm.

Robert and Carol had been homesteading their farm for the past three years, raising sheep, cows, and chickens—none were for slaughter, but instead for milk, cheese, and eggs. They sold their dairy products at the local farmer's market and also distributed them to restaurants and grocery stores throughout central Oregon. Carol also made handmade soaps using essential oils that had become quite popular not only in Oregon but up and down the West Coast. They had become budding entrepreneurs, simply out of a need to sustain their property and their livelihood.

The couple also had adopted several domestic pets they had the thrill of introducing Eli to, such as their Australian shepherd Charlie and their cats, Mitzi and Twosocks. Eli ended up having an affinity to animals seemingly since his birth; he never expressed fear, but rather an ardent curiosity and care.

Every morning Carol would take Eli to the barn, strapped to her back in a baby carrier, and he would coo while she milked the cows and sang songs by Joni Mitchell or Carole King—songs she had grown up listening to her aunt sing. "Big Yellow Taxi" was Eli's favorite; he would laugh as Carol crooned, "Don't it always seem to go… you don't know what you've got till it's gone…" If it weren't so impossible to believe, Carol would have sworn his laughter was in tune with the music.

Carol and Robert were both musicians; Carol was a singer-songwriter, Robert played guitar, and together they performed monthly at a coffee shop forty-five minutes south in Eugene, Oregon, and every weekend in the summer at the Brownsville farmer's market. Music was a hobby for them; neither had any desire to make money from it, but they both considered it an integral part of who they were and the life they lived on their farm. "It's what makes our home a home,"

Carol would say, as indeed the home always had music. Along with the home itself, Carol and Robert had inherited everything in it—which included Maggie and Mike's old turntable and records from the '70s.

Eli grew up listening to Janis Joplin, The Rolling Stones, Leonard Cohen, Van Morrison, and Carlos Santana, along with older blues acts such as Muddy Waters and Little Walter. Eli loved it all. He would dance around in his diaper, moving his body perfectly in rhythm and touting an infectious giggle.

On his third birthday, Eli was given a toy guitar as a gift. He would entertain himself for hours, strumming the strings, trying to emulate his father. Robert would place Eli's tiny little fingers in the positions to form chords, and though Eli didn't have the strength to sustain them for long, as he progressively got older, the shapes he had been taught felt intuitive—the muscle memory was there. He already had an audience—he would instruct Charlie to "Sit!" and, amazingly, Charlie would. Even Twosocks would sometimes wander by to see what all the fuss was about, though perhaps she just was engaged by the vibrating strings.

Eli's first "stage" performance was playing with his parents in the parking lot of the farmer's market at the age of five. The locals loved him; he'd stand next to his father, watching his father's hands intently in order to quickly gauge chord shifts. He couldn't play a lot of songs, but he managed to strum along to John Denver's "Take Me Home, Country Roads," and "Leaving on a Jet Plane." At the end of each song, he would take a bow, just as he saw musical performers do on TV, which his parents occasionally allowed him to watch.

Eli's musical and artistic talents were nurtured on the farm by both his parents, as was his interest in nature. If Eli wasn't practicing guitar and humming along, making up his own songs, he was wandering around the farm collecting leaves, skipping rocks in the creek, and feeding the animals. Robert and Carol felt blessed to be able to offer their son what felt like to young Eli as a magical childhood—especially because they were unable to conceive another child.

By the time Eli was six years old, his parents could see that he held a real talent for music, well beyond what seemed possible for a child of his age. They had originally planned on homeschooling their son, but it became clear he may possess a propensity for achievement that would be best fostered early on by a professional. They decided to enroll him in a Montessori school in Eugene, which was a model of education that focused on the development of the child's five senses at a pace unique to each child. Teachers were quickly impressed by Eli's listening skills, and he even showed an early aptitude for mathematics. His social skills also grew to the extent that made him a very popular boy.

By age eight, Eli was already getting attention from girls; he had a charm and charisma that developed from his early experiences on stage. He knew what audiences liked; he had a natural flair for comic timing, but also an authenticity about him that drew people in. Parents of other school children would even encourage their kids to invite Eli over to play—there was something about him that even adults were intrigued by.

Eli was usually too busy to play with the other kids, however. Anyway, their games didn't interest him. He was far keener to stay at home practicing and writing music—the latter which he was doing more and more the older he got. He had a private music teacher now, who he went to see every day after school.

Under Mr. Sherrett's stewardship, Eli's talent reached great heights. He not only learned how to read and write music and play advanced guitar, but he picked up piano and harmonica. Each instrument was more than a new challenge to Eli—it was a new companion. His parents indulged his talent, rewarding his commitment to studying with gifts of new instruments. Eli didn't know it yet, but his parents' entire life savings was going to feed his education and musical talent, and they couldn't have been happier to indulge him in that way. They wanted the best for their child, and they couldn't have been prouder of their son.

Though Eli wasn't completely aware of the sacrifices his parents made for him, he loved them dearly. He was a sweet child, who regularly thanked his parents for all they did for him—the shuttling back and forth for his school and music classes, the encouragement and support they gave him. He did have to be disciplined at times—he might have to be told to conduct some chore several times before he would leave what he was doing, which sometimes appeared to be nothing. He would sit for hours, maintaining an intense gaze, but Carol and Robert had come to discover that this was when their son was at his most creative state.

Some of the chores he didn't mind doing, however. He loved spending time with the animals. When he did, he would notice subtleties in tone among the various sounds that they made that would instruct his next song. Or, if he were picking fruit, he would notice melodies in nature—the wind blowing through the trees, and how the sound differed depending on the shape of the leaves. If he were in the barn milking the cows, he would hear how the rain on the roof performed a steady beat; he would hum a melody on top of that beat and sometimes add in lyrics he created on the spot.

By the time Eli was twelve, he had transferred out of Montessori education and entered the public school system, as the school he'd attended did not go past the sixth grade. However, he proved himself academically advanced compared to other students in his new school and was placed a year ahead of other students his age. He continued with his private music lessons in addition to joining the band in school, from which he recruited a rhythm guitarist and drummer to join him in forming his first rock band, The Brownsville Rockers. Neither of the two boys came close to Eli in musical talent, but they were decent enough at keeping rhythm for Eli to focus on vocals and lead guitar.

Eli preferred to perform solo when he could, however, and asked his parents if they could help him get a gig at the coffee shop in Eugene they had played at before they became so busy with Eli's schedule. His parents arranged a show for him, and his performance drew so much attention that the local newspaper featured him as "one to watch." He was invited back to perform weekly. Eli's parents knew that no one else had ever been offered a weekly gig there before, but they did not tell their son this. They wanted him to remain humble.

What struck everyone was that typically, for an unknown artist, audiences preferred cover songs. But this boy wrote all of his own music—and the audience couldn't get enough. Eli would be approached after each show by adults asking where they could buy his music. He would apologetically reply, "Oh, I don't record or anything. I'm too young." They would laugh and say, "Well, you better. You're missing out, kid."

He'll never forget the first time he was asked for an

autograph; it was a girl around his age. She was a precocious redhead, with adorable freckles. She was the first girl Eli had ever been attracted to—he was normally so focused on his music that he didn't pay much attention to girls. He was so nervous he couldn't find any words, but he did manage to sign the paper menu she held out to him and hand it back to her.

Maybe it was her flattery that drew him in; he wasn't sure. But he knew he liked it. He felt a stiffening in his pants while he was still on stage that caused him a great deal of embarrassment. He quickly reached for a stool nearby and played the rest of his set seated, his guitar in front of the offending member. To his chagrin, he never did see that girl again; he concluded she must have been from out of town.

Friday, April 4th was a turning point for Eli. It was his sixteenth birthday, and the age brought new-found freedom for Eli and his career. He had scheduled his driver's test the morning of his birthday and was elated when he passed. He had saved up tips from his weekly gigs to purchase his first car the month before—a 1990 burgundy Chevy Celebrity wagon that felt like a tank, but it was big enough to store his gear and get him where he needed to go.

And it seemed like he needed to go everywhere. Word had gotten out that a shining new musical talent was "rising out of the wheat fields," as the Oregonian newspaper had described. The publicity had landed Eli gigs up and down the West Coast, from Seattle to San Francisco. The buzz among Portland's music scene led to a solo gig opening for Marc Cohn at the Aladdin Theater, which happened to fall on the night of his birthday. It was the first time Eli was allowed to drive himself to one of his gigs, with the stipulation that he return home right after his set.

That was the night everything changed for Eli. A representative from BayOcean Records, a major record label at the time, was in attendance. John Keystone saw massive potential in the teenage boy. He had never seen someone so young with such a keen ear, precisely controlled instrumental technique, and profound lyrics. He appeared to understand musical cadence and dissonance, as well as the world itself, to the extent that was even over the audience members' heads.

However, what was important, he noted, was that the audience loved him. The kid didn't even have a record out to sell—and he was being asked for one left and right. His looks didn't hurt, he noticed. At six-foot-three with a slender but muscular build, he was sure to grow into a sex symbol. Girls swooned over his hazel eyes and dirty blonde, wavy hair and gentle charisma. John saw an opportunity before him, and he seized it.

He waited until the end of Eli's set before asking for an introduction to the boy from the theater's manager, who had led him backstage to the green room.

"Eli, good evening. I'm John Keystone, with BayOcean Records."

Eli swallowed, trying to cover his dry mouth. BayOcean was the label that helped propel some of his favorite rock artists into the international spotlight.

"Good evening, sir. It's a pleasure to meet you." Eli shook John's hand with his sweaty palm.

"That was a great performance you gave out there tonight."

"Thank you. Thank you very much, that means a lot."

"Do you have anyone representing you?"

"Not yet, sir. My parents manage my tour schedule and promotion."

"I see. Are you aware, Eli, that you could be sellin venues far greater than this theater here, as the headlining a

"I can only dream."

"It doesn't have to be only a dream. How old are you, son?"

"I turned sixteen today, sir."

"Really? Happy birthday. Are you attending school?"

"Yes. I am a junior in high school, in Brownsville. I am driving back home now, in fact."

"Well, I'll tell you what, Eli. Here's my card. Call me as soon as you get back to Brownsville. I've got a deal to offer you."

"I will, sir. I promise you."

"I'll hold you to that," John winked and gracefully exited from backstage.

Eli stood staring at the business card in his hand, only half believing what had just happened.

CHAPTER FIVE

-----⬡-----

A RISING STAR

It was after midnight when Eli returned home, and his parents were already in bed. He contemplated calling Mr. Keystone that night, but he didn't want to appear too anxious, nor did he wish to wake his parents. He wanted to find out the man's offer before he told his parents about it. I'll call first thing tomorrow, he decided. He didn't sleep much that night; he could sense his life was about to change in a very pivotal way.

He welcomed the change. He had grown increasingly discontent with his life in Brownsville; he didn't have any friends in town, aside from the guys in his band. He was meeting them later that night at Lucky Lanes, the town's bowling alley. The guys had insisted they do something for his birthday, but Eli didn't much want to attend. He knew that the gathering would likely turn into a drink fest behind the dumpster out back. Eli wasn't much into drinking, but the other kids in school were, and sometimes he went along with it just to avoid having to defend his lack of interest.

The kids at school already thought he was "weird," not only because he was so smart, but because he never dated any of the girls in their class. It wasn't for lack of physical attraction, but lack of emotional connection that made Eli largely ignore the female population at his high school. He couldn't believe the stupid shit they talked about. He'd had a girlfriend once—for one month. Pamela, the class homecoming queen.

She'd feigned interest in his musings in the beginning, but after two weeks of nodding in agreement as he talked about, "the musical composition of air versus water," she finally admitted, "My god, Eli, why can't you just be normal?! You're the cutest guy in our class; you could have any girl you want. The other boys are dying to get into a girl's pants and can't, and you could—but you prefer to babble on and on about woo-woo stuff without so much as ever kissing me. What is wrong with you?!"

Eli was, honestly, beginning to wonder if there was something wrong with him. He felt so different than all the other kids in school. All he could think about was music. He didn't necessarily want to be a rock star—even saying that phrase made him feel ridiculous—but he wanted to be surrounded by people who got him. He was tired of having to explain mathematical and rhythmic concepts to other people that to him felt so damn obvious. But there might be a way out; if John Keystone offered him a record deal with BayOcean…

He had dreamed about such a circumstance for the past few years. In his dream, he pictured himself on tour not only along the West Coast, but the Midwest and the South. He wanted to cruise the entire length of Highway 61—the "Blues Highway"—that Bob Dylan had written about. He saw himself stopping to play in St. Paul, St. Louis, Memphis, and Clarksdale, Mississippi—where Robert Johnson purportedly sold his soul to the devil—all the way to New Orleans.

He wanted to study the roots of not only blues but jazz—especially the "trad jazz" revival movement that included elements of the Chicago blues and Dixieland jazz style he loved so much. Chicago…he couldn't wait to play Chicago—the city that was greatly responsible for the future creation of rock and roll.

And then…then he would explore the East Coast jazz scene. He couldn't get enough of the Afro-Cuban clave beats that had developed out of New York City by Dizzy Gillespie and percussionist Chano Pozo from Cuba. There was so much to see, so much to experience! Oregon was not enough for him anymore. He loved being surrounded by nature as a boy and was greatly inspired by his observations on the farm, but he longed for more.

Maybe John Keystone would be the answer to his prayers. He sat at the foot of his bed, his bedroom door shut. He could hear his parents outside feeding the animals, but he didn't want to take any chances of being overheard should one of them enter the house. He took a final deep breath before dialing the number on the business card. The phone rang three times.

"John Keystone."

"Yes, hi, sir. This is Eli Evans; we met last…"

"I remember. Nice to hear from you, Eli. I'm glad you called. Again, great show last night."

"Thank you."

"Now tell me, what are your plans for the future?"

"To keep playing and studying."

"The only education you need, son, is on the road."

Eli was taken aback a bit by John's statement. He expected him to say what all adults were telling him: "Finish high school, get a degree, and you can get a good job teaching music."

"Have you thought about making a record?"

"I think about it every day. I haven't had much time though, aside from my school work and gigs on the weekends."

"That's all about to change."

"In what regard, sir?"

"I'm prepared to offer you a deal, Eli. I want to get your music out there. You have something special that the public deserves to hear. It will require hard work on your part, though. Are you prepared for that?"

"I've been working hard my whole life, sir. I grew up on a farm."

John laughed, "Well, the music business is different, but I'll take it. What I'd need from you is a commitment to doing what it takes—long hours on the road, long hours in the studio, determination, and passion for not just music, but money. Do you want to be a rich man, Eli?"

"I want to be successful."

"Success and money are the same things, Eli. At least in the music business. People dig what you put out; you sell records, you make money. How bad do you want to make music that people dig?"

"I live for it."

"Good. If you commit to doing that for me, I'm willing to make you an offer no musician in their right mind would refuse. We usually offer new artists one-year contracts, but you have something special, Eli. We believe you will go far, and we want to invest in you for the long term. If you sign with BayOcean for the next five years, we will offer you an up-front signing bonus of $1 million."

Eli wasn't sure he heard him right.

"I'm sorry, how much did you just say? You've got to be kidding, right?"

"One million dollars, Eli. It's no joke. I believe in you. But to sign with us, you'd have to work hard for us—which means you won't be able to go to school. You'll have to commit to recording and promoting your music. We will keep you busy touring all over the world, Eli. Have you been to Europe before?"

"In my dreams."

John laughed again, "Well, your dreams are about to come true, Eli. But here's the deal—you need to act fast. Summer is approaching, which is peak touring season, and we need to get you a record made before that. Can you and someone able to sign for you make it down to L.A. next Tuesday? We'll get the contract written up, introduce you to our studio musicians, and we can begin working with some of that material I heard you perform in Portland."

"Next Tuesday? I have school until June, sir."

"June is too late, Eli. It's now or never. You can continue with your current plan, attend high school for another year, go to college, and end up in a stuffy old classroom teaching other people how to succeed in music until you're too old to make anything of value yourself. Or you can make your own music, live by your own rules, see the world, and have the chance to be a star yourself. The option is yours, Eli—and because you're under eighteen, of course, at least one of your parents will have to be on board, too."

Eli's heart was racing, and his mind was going a mile a minute… no other kid at school had ever been offered such an opportunity. BayOcean Records was on the phone…offering him $1 million! It felt like a dream. How could this be real? He was just a farm kid from Brownsville, Oregon. But how the heck was he supposed to get his parents to agree to quit school? Never mind, he would find a way to convince them.

"Yes, sir. We will be there."

"Good. You've made me a very happy man, Eli. And I will make you a very successful musician."

John gave Eli the details of when and where to meet him on Monday.

"Bring all of your songs. You don't need to bring your instruments—we have Fender Stratocasters, Gibson Flying V's and everything in between."

Eli swallowed. These were the instruments artists such as Jimi Hendrix, Lenny Kravitz, and Stevie Ray Vaughn played.

"I can't wait, sir."

"We look forward to seeing you then. The whole town will know your name, Eli."

"They already do."

"Ha! I suppose that's true. I forgot how small your town is. Well, never mind; the whole world will know your name, Eli."

Eli hadn't given much energy to ego before, but he liked the sound of that.

"See you Monday." John hung up.

Eli wiped the sweat from his palms on his bedcover and contemplated a strategy to convince his parents to agree with him that this was the opportunity of a lifetime.

ELI RECLINED ON THE BLACK LEATHER COUCH INSIDE HIS custom-made Senators tour bus. He'd spent more days on that bus in the past four years than he had in his L.A. apartment, or even a hotel. The first tour he embarked on lasted nine months, and this next tour would run for a full year. He appeared to live a life of luxury, and in some ways, he did—but it was certainly not on his terms, as he'd been promised.

He'd been with BayOcean for just under five years; he had four months remaining on his contract, and he couldn't wait to get out. Sure, they had given him a lot. He started his career opening for such acts as Eric Clapton, Bruce Springsteen, and the Rolling Stones. The fucking Rolling Stones, sometimes he still couldn't believe it. But he'd paid a heavy price.

He had been an eager and naïve sixteen-year-old when he left Brownsville two days after his birthday to drive to L.A. It had been easier to convince his parents to enter into the contract than he'd expected, but that was because—for the first time in his life—he was recklessly dishonest with them. His parents recognized the incredible opportunity before him and agreed that likely all three of them would regret it if they didn't see where it could lead—but his parents thought they had agreed to a one-year contract for their son.

Eli had convinced them that since he'd skipped a grade in school, it would be a fair reward for his hard work to give his musical career one year of attention. After that year, Eli promised he would return to school to graduate high school at age eighteen and pursue higher education—using the $1 million sign-on bonus to fund college.

When Eli sat around the conference table with his parents in Los Angeles and several representatives from BayOcean Records, no one brought attention to the fine print of the contract. Eli had been led to believe by John Keystone that a five-year contract was far more valuable than a one-year contract, and he was sure his parents would agree after what he was convinced would be a successful first year of his musical career—but he suspected, rightfully so, that they would not agree at this time.

He had felt bad for having misled his parents, of course. It was the first time he'd lied to his parents about anything substantial. They were devastated when they found out, to put it bluntly. They were disappointed in their son and disappointed in themselves for having gotten so caught up in the excitement of the offer that they didn't consult a lawyer to review the contract. Eli, as well, learned a very hard lesson. He'd locked himself into a five-year contract with only a 1% royalty rate.

His career, however, took off immediately. Eli's first headlining tour grossed over $75 million; he sold 1.28 million copies of his first record, Starry Nights, yet he received mere pennies in payment. Not only had he accepted a low royalty rate, but he had also entirely missed the clause in the contract that stated the record label was allowed to recoup its expenses through royalty "deductions"—which included recording costs, video production costs, album packaging, touring costs, and the label owners' salaries and benefits.

John Keystone—even the name made him cringe—had told him he'd be a rich man...what a joke. Sure, Eli had been given the $1 million upfront bonus he'd been promised, but most of that money went towards the beachside Los Angeles apartment that sat empty most of the year, and a few impulse buys—an Aston Martin he rarely had time to drive, a Jetten 40 Classic private yacht he had even less opportunity to enjoy, and his cherished Gibson Les Paul and Fender Telecaster guitars.

Thankfully, John Keystone was no longer his manager; he'd been fired from BayOcean within Eli's first year with the label, due to a lawsuit another artist had filed against him and won. But Eli was still held to the terms of his own contract. He liked his new manager well enough, but he was not offered the creative liberty that he craved.

He was kept incredibly busy—he'd released two albums now, and he was embarking on the second week of his second headlining tour in promotion of the latter, Road Rage. It wasn't just touring that was exhausting—it was all the damn interviews and media appearances he was expected to do. They had been fun in the beginning, but now he just went through the motions of telling them what he knew they wanted to hear. What they published wouldn't even be true to what he said, he finally figured out.

Fucking media, Eli thought to himself. One of the hardest lifestyle changes his newfound fame had brought him was a loss of privacy. Cameras were everywhere; he could hardly take a piss without someone whipping out a lens. He remembered using a bathroom stall at a roadside dive during a band pit-stop in Indianapolis when someone—a fan or a journalist, who knows—stretched a camera under the stall and snapped a picture of him halfway through his business. The shot ended up going viral, of course.

Anyway, he chalked those situations up to the price he had to pay to get his music out to the masses. The reception he received by the fans for his music made the loss of his privacy, and to some extent even his identity, worth it.

Tonight, would be no exception. He was heading to Portland, Oregon, where he would play before a sold-out crowd. He had outgrown the Aladdin Theater, however. This show would be at a sports arena. The show was incredibly important to him. His parents would be there.

Eli's contact with his parents over the last four years had been minimal. He had visited them twice in his first year under contract and only once since. He called them every few weeks, but the conversations were short, and he was disengaged. He didn't have the time, and he didn't have the desire to see how much he'd crushed their hearts by lying and not finishing school—nor did he wish for them to know more about who he was becoming.

To maintain the energy, he needed to perform so many nights in a row, he would self-medicate each night with nicotine and caffeine before a show, and marijuana and sleeping pills after the backstage high wore off. Some of his bandmates took hard drugs, but Eli just wanted to stick with what he needed to stay alert and to decompress. He had heard stories of too many great musicians falling by the wayside after succumbing to heavy drugs and alcohol—Jim Morrison, Jimi Hendrix, and Janis Joplin, to name a few. Though he had dabbled with ecstasy a couple of times and acid once, he was determined to stay clear of anything that might impair or affect his future. He didn't want to die young. If Bob Dylan and Keith Richards could still be playing in their sixties, he could, too.

Technically, Eli was still underage even to drink, but that sort of thing was overlooked in the industry. His parents, on the other hand, might care about what everyone else cared less about. Aside from learning about his drinking or smoking, however, Eli knew what hurt his parents even more. It was that when he was with them, he wasn't really with them. They'd comment on the faraway look in his eyes. When they shared what was going on in their lives or back at the farm, it was not hard for them to notice his lack of interest.

They were "country folk" to him now, they knew. He had seen life—the bustling club scene in New York City's Greenwich Village, the dirty streets of the Tree in New Orleans, the edgy yet trendy re-envisioning of London's SoHo district. He couldn't have felt further away from Brownsville both physically and emotionally over the past several years.

His parents were proud of his music and proud of his accomplishments, but they missed their son. They missed the sweet nature he'd held as a child and even as a young teenager. He had become so emotionally distant; they heard it in his voice when they managed to talk on the phone. They had forgiven him for not finishing high school and going to college. But Eli nonetheless felt they were disappointed in him—in his disengagement with the family, and the community that had nurtured him.

That speculation shook him now. He was feeling nostalgic, and he didn't like it. This would be the first headlining gig his parents would see him perform. They had seen him open for a few shows up and down the West Coast, but his first headlining tour had mostly taken place on the East Coast and Europe—he had quite a following in England and Germany, in particular. He hated to admit how much he wanted his parents' approval, not just of his music—he had that already—but who he was. He feared they'd never truly understand why he had to leave.

He'd be embarrassed for them to see how he lived now. Looking around the bus, he saw pill containers, empty liquor bottles, and even some chick's panties that had been left there the night before. The pill containers weren't his, but the liquor bottles he was partially responsible for, and the panties entirely. It gets lonely on the road; he justified to himself. He couldn't even remember her name now. Anyway, none of the girls he met on the road meant anything to him. They adored him, and that felt nice. They liked his music, sure. Did they know anything about who he really was? Absolutely not. He was beginning to forget who he was himself or to wonder if he ever really knew.

I'm a musician. He tried that one on. Well, duh. I'm an entertainer. Yes, that too. I'm a businessman. He didn't consider himself the latter, yet, but he was going to. When his contract ended, he was going to start his own record label. He was sick of the bullshit he'd had to put up with. He wanted to choose his own band members, entirely orchestrate his own songs, and choose where and when he would play. He had developed a solid following over the past few years and sold a lot of records, but he knew he could do even better.

He had so many ideas—he continued to study mathematical formulas after he left school, and he was convinced he was onto a groundbreaking realization that, when applied to music, would alter the course of contemporary blues and neo jazz-hop. But he'd be damned if he would tell anyone from BayOcean about it—they'd either crush the idea from the start or promote it and make millions off of it in his place. He was saving it for later.

He had to let this tour run its course first. In a couple of hours, they'd be in Portland. He was more anxious than usual. He typically didn't drink before a show, but he was already feeling edgy. He poured himself a gin and tonic and sat back, watching the I-5 highway roll by. They had just passed Eugene, Oregon, which meant Brownsville was just up the road. They weren't stopping in the town, but he was close enough to it for familiar memories to emerge.

He had forgotten how beautiful the area was. Tall Ponderosa pines and Douglas firs filled his field of vision. They were mostly amid farmland, but the Willamette National Forest could be seen not far away to the east. He didn't have to step outside to remember the scent of the pine and the ripple of the Caledonia River that ran right through his parents' property. He'd spent so many joyful days there as a child; he recalled now, how the land and the animals there had inspired much of his early music. He'd gotten a lot more experimental since then, but the roots of his music remained based in nature.

Nothing happens there, though. Eli shook himself out of his trance. Nobody there understood me.

As he relaxed into his drink, he closed his eyes and saw visions of his teenage years. "Why can't you just be normal?" The words Pamela had once said to him were repeated many times over the years by other peers… "Just take a hit, man. It's only pot. Nothing is going to happen. Don't be such a pussy." At the time, he never touched marijuana or any of the drugs the kids at school were doing.

Eli glanced at a bud on the counter leftover from the night before. "If only they could see me now," he laughed in spite of himself, though he really didn't find the situation humorous. He wished he didn't have to take any substance… he didn't even like drinking all that much, but the habit had developed nevertheless, through his effort to fit in on the road. He discovered, however, that it not only helped him fit in, it helped him forget.

He forgot about how much he knew he had disappointed his parents. He forgot about all the women he slept with on the road, who were hurt when they never heard from him again. He forgot about his yearning to answer that one stupid question, "Who the hell am I?"

"Eli! Dude, wake up. We're in Portland," Eli's drummer, Geoffrey, kicked Eli's foot on his way off the bus. What? Already? He didn't realize he'd fallen asleep. Fuck. He'd planned to shave, too. His parents would be meeting him shortly. He felt dizzy as he stood up, and stumbled slightly on his way to the bathroom.

He tried to freshen up. He splashed his face with cold water, lathered some Caswell Massey bath soap in his hands and quickly scrubbed his face. He brushed his teeth, too, but he knew he couldn't extinguish the slight smell of alcohol from his breath.

Geoffrey stuck his head back through the bus door, "Eli! There's someone out here to see you.

Says she's your mom?"

Shit shit.

He threw on a fresh shirt, stuffed the empty bottles and leftover Buds in the cabinet, just in case, put on a smile, and stepped down off the bus.

"Mother, nice to see you," Eli walked over and gently hugged her.

"Eli," was all she managed to say before tears came to his mother's eyes. He didn't know what to say himself. He had missed her…more than he'd realized. But he was embarrassed by his condition; he could pass for a homeless person if he weren't wearing designer brands. She didn't bring it up, though.

"Where's dad?"

"He's parking the car. It's a madhouse out there."

"Is it?"

"Everyone wants to see my boy. They barely let me back here…"

"Really? I had called ahead. They were supposed to get you both backstage passes."

"Well, they said we weren't on the list."

"Sorry," Eli was pretty sure he had called in advance. Come to think of it, maybe he had forgotten.

"Son!"

Eli turned around to see his father walking swiftly over to him. He was ashamed to admit that he was embarrassed by his father's cowboy hat and jeans. He still looked like a farmer.

"Dad, hello," Eli extended his arm for a handshake, but his father pulled him in for a hug. Eli wished he hadn't; it was impossible to cover up his body stench and the smell of his breath.

His dad pulled back. Like his wife, he said nothing. Eli imagined the disappointment they must feel. It hit his heart harder than any harsh words could have.

"So, you're a big deal around here, huh?" his father's tone was lighthearted.

"Heh. Yeah, I guess so," Eli looked down; he felt uncomfortable with all the flattery around his parents.

"It's good to see you, Son," his dad reflected awkwardly.

"Yeah, it's good to see you too, Dad." The three of them stood silently for a few moments, taking each other and their environment.

A flurry of activity surrounded them; the stage crew was unloading their equipment, catering was being set up under a tent, and security was ushering away fans on the other side of the fence. They weren't supposed to be back by the bus, but somehow there was always a group that made their way to places they weren't supposed to be.

"Eli! We love you!"

"Would you sign this for me?"

"Eli! Eli! Eli!"

"Sign my boob!"

"Sorry," Eli apologized to his parents. "This is my life now."

"We see that," his dad answered quietly, but without judgment.

"Are you happy, Eli?" his mother asked.

"I'm happier than I would be on the farm," the words left Eli's mouth before he had a chance to consider how they must sound.

"I see," his mother's eyes brimmed with tears again.

"Oh, no, mom, I didn't mean it like that. I mean, I'm glad I get to travel. I'm glad I get to play music. I was happy on the farm, too. I just needed more. Or something different, I guess."

"I understand."

Eli didn't think she did.

"I'm excited for you to see the show tonight. Have you heard my new album?"

"Yes, we have. It doesn't sound like you."

"Well, I mean, it's a version of me, anyway. I wrote all the songs. I'd write them differently if they let me, but I'm still proud of it."

"We're proud of you, you know," his dad added.

Eli's heart skipped a beat. "You are?"

"Yes, of course."

"We miss you, Eli," Eli's mom added.

Eli felt he should say the same, but the words caught in his throat. "I've got to get ready for the show. I'll look for you out there, okay?"

"Okay."

Eli turned and climbed back onto the bus.

"We love you!" his mother called after him, but he didn't hear.

A few hours later, after the band rehearsal and after the opening act, Eli walked onstage to thundering applause.

"Eli! Eli! Eli!" the room was chanting. He felt so alive; the room loved him. More than Berlin, more than London. He got high off the feeling; if he could communicate so deeply through music that wasn't even a full expression of who he was, imagine what he could convey to a crowd through the songs he was working on…the ones he would release on his own label.

The lights went up in a flash of color; beams of reds and blues burst onto the stage backdrop. Eli opened with a fierce guitar riff, heightened in energy by perfectly timed drum emphasis that left the audience screaming, the women crying.

Eli's eyes landed on his parents, in the front row. At least he'd gotten their tickets right. His mom seemed to struggle with the loud noise; she wore earplugs, but her face still cringed with all the screaming. His dad held a solemn expression; a mixture of pride in his eyes, and something else… disappointment? Eli felt sure of it. That realization hurt. It hurt so fucking bad.

Petra Nicoll

CHAPTER SIX

BURN OUT

Eli slowly and deliberately extinguished his cigarette, tapping it gently in the checkered ashtray on the bedside table in his Memphis hotel room. He watched as each red speck of light died out, leaving only one single spark remaining.

It's not really red, Eli thought. It's more of a…burnt sienna. Eli pondered the details of the hue for several moments. Hey, that's a great name for my next album. Burnt Sienna.

For a terrifying instant, Eli felt a chilling wave rush through him as he thought. If I make it until then. He didn't want to entertain that thought, so he quickly brushed it aside. But a minute later, it came back. What if this is my last tour? What if I never record again?

"I don't know what will happen now..." a familiar voice came through the TV set.

Eli looked up from his cigarette and fixed his gaze upon the TV. It was April 3, 2016, the 48th anniversary of Martin Luther King's final speech at the Mason Temple in Memphis, and the local news station was airing its entirety in remembrance.

The Mason Temple, in fact, was merely two miles up the road from Eli's room for the night at The Peabody Hotel.

"We've got some difficult days ahead. But it really doesn't matter with me now, because I've been to the mountaintop."

So, have I, Eli thought.

"Like anybody, I would like to live a long life. Longevity has its place. But I'm not concerned about that now. I just want to do God's will. And He's allowed me to go up to the mountain. And I've looked over. And I've seen the Promised Land. I may not get there with you. But I want you to know tonight, that we, as a people, will get to the promised land!"

Ha! We still haven't made it there. Eli sighed as he stood to turn off the TV.

He would turn twenty-four years old in just over an hour. His band had urged him to celebrate down on Beale Street with them, but he'd insisted on staying at the hotel.

"I want to be alone," he'd asserted.

"Come on, man. The music is killer, the women are hot, we finally have a night off between gigs, it's about to be your birthday, and you're going to stay at the hotel?!"

"Yes, I am," Eli's usual good humor was not present that night. "You guys have fun."

"Suit yourself," the guys wandered off down the hall singing boisterously, "Happy birthday dear Eli…"

Happy birthday to me. Eli walked to the window and peered down on the city below.

He felt impossibly young and prematurely old at the same time. Professionally, no one else on earth had achieved what he had at his age—or any age, for that matter. Since he left his contract with BayOcean and began his own label, Apocalyptic, he sold 29 million copies of the label's first release, Ventilate;

and eight months into his promotional tour for the label's second release, Jaded, he had already sold 34 million copies.

This would be his longest tour yet; his manager had insisted on an eighteen-month, worldwide run to maximize exposure. He felt certain that, at this pace, Eli's latest album would surpass the success of Michael Jackson's Thriller. Since its release, the album had spent thirty-two weeks at number one on the Billboard charts. It also held the record for worldwide digital sales.

Album sales aside, Ventilate had been awarded twelve Grammy Awards, twenty-one American Music Awards, and twenty-three Billboard Music Awards. At age twenty-three, Eli was inducted into the Songwriters Hall of Fame. He had done everything right since he broke with his first label; he'd hired top lawyers to ensure he held exclusive rights to all of his music, which had since been featured on countless TV shows, Academy Award-winning movies, commercials and more.

There was no iconic music venue in the world he hadn't sold out—Red Rocks amphitheater in Colorado, the Ryman Auditorium in Nashville, the National Centre for the Performing Arts in Beijing, Royal Albert Hall in London, Palacio de Bellas Artes in Mexico City, the Sydney Opera House in Australia…all of these experiences had been significantly impactful to Eli at the time. Lately, however, it had become difficult to impress him.

Money, prestige, the glitz and the glamor…he had seen it all. He'd had just as many women drop diamonds in his pockets at after-parties as he had women throw bras at his feet while onstage. Everyone wanted a piece of him—whether it be a walk down the aisle or a quickie they could brag to their friends about.

For a while, he'd let himself indulge in the pleasures that came along with being not just a rock star but a sex symbol; People Magazine had labeled him "Sexiest Man Alive" the year before, which felt ridiculous to him but earned him an additional influx of groupies. He'd had no serious relationship ever in his life, however. To maintain a relationship on the road would hardly have been possible.

He'd met a few women he was interested in, for sure. He'd had brief but meaningful exchanges with a film producer he'd met in Paris, a dancer he'd seen perform on the streets of Brussels, and a horse trainer he'd met in Maryland while filming a music video. But always, he'd needed to fulfill expectations to be somewhere else before anything deeper could evolve. Perhaps he preferred it that way. The level of intensity was always greater when he knew a relationship was temporary.

Despite his regular and willful participation in a romp on the bus or in a hotel room after a gig, he would never date a fan. He could never trust their intentions. He'd had pictures and oft-exaggerated stories plastered across media outlets from all too eager to share fans. He'd been accused of bringing a fifteen-year-old girl onto his bus, which he had—but nothing had happened before he found out how old she was and immediately called her a cab to get the hell out of there. The media had a heyday with that story, regardless; it took his PR agent several months to clear his name.

Then there were the girls who didn't even want sex; they just wanted his money. He'd heard every sob story under the sun. He believed them in the beginning; he'd written more checks than he could remember and doled out cash to many strangers who told him of their troubles. He was still generous, but lately, he'd taken to only writing checks to charities.

He also performed a charity concert every year in support of victims of human trafficking. *That must make up for all the women on the road I must have hurt over the years,* Eli justified. *But they've hurt me, too,* he considered.

He may have enjoyed their bodies and been pleased they'd enjoyed his…but they'd never be able to see passed who they thought he was, Eli the rock star! Eli, the sexiest man alive! The paparazzi and the fans alike treated him like he was immortal. Like he was owned by them. They would never know his pain, the persistent lack of purpose he felt.

They would know his numbers…

The number of records sold.

The number of hits he had.

The number of gigs he'd played.

The number of dollars he made.

Just the day before, his manager had shown him the recently published Forbes list of the 100 highest-paid celebrities, which estimated his net worth to be close to five billion dollars. But Eli could have cared less about that. So, what? They were just numbers.

Numbers used to matter so much to me, Eli recalled.

His latest album, in fact, had been the culmination of several years spent analyzing sequences of numbers in music. He had studied the Fibonacci sequence—an integer sequence where each number is the sum of the two preceding numbers. He saw early on that there was a connection between this mathematical sequence and the composition of artwork—in his case, music.

Eli also learned about the Golden Ratio—a number found by dividing a line into two parts so that the longer part divided by the smaller part is also equal to the whole length divided by the longer part. Subconsciously, Eli understood even as a small child that these sequences and ratios were abundant in nature—he observed the intricate designs in the petals of lilies, the seed heads of sunflowers, and the seed pods of pine cones. He was mesmerized by the spiral formation in shells and spider webs…wherever he looked, he seemed to find the same design.

He saw how the sequence would underlie particular musical intervals and compositions—and even noticed the golden ratio in the design of the highest quality musical instruments. No one had taught him these principals; he never knew they had been studied or had names. When he tried to express what he saw and understood in grade school, even his teachers had looked confused. His peers laughed at him.

"What are you smoking?" he remembered being asked by one of his high school bandmates. He didn't try to explain it further—with anyone, in fact—until he interviewed musicians trying out for his band after he broke with his first label. To even be considered, they had to understand what these numbers meant. To be hired, they needed to demonstrate that they could compose a new piece off the cuff, using those sequences and ratios.

Eli was known in the business for being slightly eccentric. He didn't consider himself difficult to work with, but he did hold high, and sometimes ambiguous, expectations.

"If they are right for the band, my expectations aren't ambiguous at all," he would say.

He had a surefire way of testing that theory. The guys made fun of him, but it worked well. If they were in session and weren't picking up on what Eli was wanting, he would explain, "You guys are playing like shrubs. I want you to play like trees."

If they looked at him with blank faces or didn't correct their mistake, Eli would know they were not a good fit for the band.

Eli made sure his band members were intellectually superior, technically exceptional, and remarkably disciplined. He did not tolerate the use of hard drugs by any member; casual drinking and marijuana were allowed so long as they didn't impair their performance, but if any other substance were found or used, their position with the band (and their generous paycheck) was gone.

In fact, that's what had brought him and the band to Memphis. They'd had to let their bass player go after he'd begun showing visible signs of cocaine use. Eli needed to find a replacement fast, and a blues competition had taken place the day before that was a ripe feeding ground for talent.

The day had been successful; he'd interviewed and held a session with a guy from Birmingham he was excited about. He'll fit in well with our gang of crazies. Eli smiled as he thought of his band members, their birthday cheer finally having faded down the hall. He had built a tribe of good people around him. He had been burned by many, but once he learned how the business worked, he used his sharpened intuition to weed out those he felt would become toxic.

He could see the roof of Sun Studio from his perch high above the city. Elvis had recorded there…Johnny Cash, U2, John Mellencamp. He had recorded there a few years before, on a tribute album to B.B. King. "The Blues Highway," Eli whispered to himself. He could see it from there, too. It went right through the core of the city. He'd traveled the whole highway, just as he'd dreamed of while still in high school. John Keystone had been right about one thing—his dreams would come true.

A blessing and a curse, Eli thought. What is there left to dream of now?

"I've been to the mountaintop…" Eli repeated the words he'd heard on TV. I just want to do God's will. The latter line returned to him now; he had never heard it before as part of the speech.

"Hmmph. God's will. I don't know about that," Eli had never dismissed the possible existence of God, but he hadn't paid much thought or attention to how the role of God might play out in his own life.

But tonight, he was feeling thoughtful. Maybe a little desperate.

"Alright, God. If you're out there, show me a sign. Tell me what I'm here for. If all of this has a purpose, I need to know, because otherwise, I see no point in continuing with this lifestyle. I'm tired. So, fucking tired. There has to be more than all this…"

Eli waited several minutes for something to happen—he didn't exactly know what—only to be disappointed.

"Yeah, that's what I thought." Eli shrugged. For once in what must have been years, he went to bed before midnight.

ELI WOKE TO A SUDDEN KNOCK ON THE DOOR AT 8 A.M. THE next morning.

"Eil! Are you up? We've gotta go." Russ, his manager, called through the door.

Eli raised his arms above his head and stretched his feet out. Normally he dreaded this moment; mornings were not his favorite time of day. But today he felt rested; slightly optimistic about the day, even.

I should go to bed early more often, he thought.

"Yeah. Give me a few minutes."

"Okay, we'll be in the lobby. Don't be late. Flight's leaving in an hour."

"Got it. I'll be down."

Eli threw back the covers and stood to stretch. He glanced at the clock, "I've got time for coffee," he said to himself.

He started a pot and stepped into the shower for a quick rinse.

He was flying to San Francisco that morning for an interview with some magazine. Pop Candy…Sugar Pop…he couldn't remember the name for sure. All media publications ran together in his mind. They all were equally dull. They didn't care about the music; they didn't even understand it. They just wanted to know who was sleeping with who or to dig up whatever scandal they could that would make their ratings soar.

Letting the water flow off his body, Eli imagined the residue of road life washing down the drain. The dirt, the smoke, the diesel, the buzz, the girls, the cameras, the crowds…

He was glad to be headed back to the West Coast. Really, he wanted to be in Oregon. April in the Northwest was his favorite time of year; he didn't realize how special it was until he left. No other place he'd visited in spring had quite the dynamic flower show that Oregon displayed. If you could survive all that rain, the reward was sweet.

I suppose I miss my parents, too, Eli admitted to himself as he stepped out of the shower.

As if on cue, Eli's phone rang. "Mom," it read. He contemplated if he should answer. He had to hurry. I suppose I have time to talk while I drink my coffee, he concluded.

"Hello?"

"Eli. Happy birthday!"

"Thanks, Mom."

"Dad's here, too."

"Happy birthday, Son!" his father's voice rang through.

"Thanks, Dad. How are you guys?"

"We're fine. Just wanted you to know we're thinking of you. Where are you, anyway?"

"Memphis. But I'm heading to San Francisco in a bit here."

"Don't forget to wear flowers in your hair."

"What?"

"Never mind. Stupid joke," his mom recoiled.

They're so corny, Eli thought to himself, but with a somewhat endearing sensation. He took a sip of his coffee.

"How are you, Eli?"

"Fine, fine. I guess a little bit busy."

"We know, we know. Always got somewhere to be. Listen, we won't keep you, but we want to wish you a happy birthday, and we hope you take some time off for yourself today."

"For myself?" Eli laughed. "Well, let's see. I took the night off last night. Today I've got a media gig and then rehearsal with the band. We brought a new guy on board yesterday, and we need him to be ready for our next gig."

"Nice, congratulations. We hope he works out for you."

"Thanks."

"Alright, Eli, do what you gotta do. Nice to hear your voice."

"Thanks, Dad, nice to hear from you both, too."

"We'll talk another time," his mom suggested. "Bye, Eli."

"Sure, sounds good," Eli paused. "Wait, are you still there?"

"Yes, we're here."

"How are things at the farm?"

"Good, they're good. Spring has sprung. Everything is in bloom—camas, bleeding hearts, trillium. Rhododendrons should be coming in shortly. It's beautiful, Eli. You should see it."

Eli's mom's last words rang in his head and his heart. "I'd like that, Mom. I really would."

"We hope to see you soon, Son."

"Yeah. Me too. Okay, I've got to go. Thanks for calling."

"You bet. Happy birthday again."

"Cheers," Eli hung up, took a swig of his coffee, and quickly dressed. Gathering his suitcase, he charged down the hall to the elevator. "Here I go again," he whispered to himself.

ELI'S LIMO PULLED UP TO THE CURB JUST OUTSIDE THE MAGA-zine's building in downtown San Francisco. Typically, media outlets just wanted to interview Eli, but this time he'd insisted they agree to interview the whole band.

One by one, the guys got out. Security guards ushered them to the front door. Their arrival must have been leaked because already swarms of fans engulfed them.

"Eli! Ohmigod!!!"

Eli did not mean to appear ungrateful; sometimes he was just tired of all the fuss. Today, especially, as he was dealing with an intense discomfort in his back that had developed seemingly out of nowhere while on stage a few nights before. The pain made him extra cranky. He tucked his head down and continued straight toward the entrance.

"Excuse me, Mr. Evans, would you say a few words about your current tour?" a microphone was shoved in Eli's face.

"Talk to him," Eli gestured towards his manager.

Eli and his band members were quickly ushered inside,

onto the elevator, and led to the sixteenth floor.

"Welcome, gentlemen, thank you for coming. Right this way," the receptionist greeted them.

The band was settled in a conference room down the hall, adorned with photos of celebrities who had graced issues of the magazine. A cold Pellegrino awaited each place setting.

A blonde, slender woman in her mid-twenties appeared, wearing a V-neck red blouse and black and white polka dot skirt.

"Good afternoon, everyone. Glad you are here. We know you all are busy, so let's not waste any time. I'll get going with the questions. Eli, we'll start with you."

Surprise, surprise, Eli thought.

"Our team hasn't been able to stop playing your new record. Track four, especially—that song always grabs our attention."

Hmm. Maybe these people do care about the music.

"There's a line in the song where you say, 'You came to me in a dream last night, your body bejeweled by drops of crystalline sweat. You reminded me of summer lilies draped in dew, except after the sun you evaporated, too.' Now, we're all just dying to know—who is this song about?!"

Of course, they'd ask about the only love song on my record, Eli thought. It wasn't even a real love song—it wasn't about anyone he knew. It was about the illusion of a woman— someone he wanted but couldn't quite get to know…only in real life; it was because he would leave, not her. How could he explain that? Well, he could, but did he want to? No. He did not.

"Yes, my song Transitory. It's actually about my car."

"What? Your car?" she giggled.

"Yeah. One morning, I saw it was covered in dew. She's a beautiful thing, though. Purrs like a cat. But I hardly get to drive her, because I'm on the road all the time."

"Ohmigosh, that is so funny!"

"Haha yeah, I suppose it is," Eli feigned a laugh, and through a sideways glance noticed his drummer trying not to chuckle.

"Okay, next question. You looked stunning at your performance at the Grammys in February. Who were you wearing?"

"Who?" Eli had been asked the question before, but it never failed to catch him. He was also distracted by a sudden spasm in his back. He shifted in his seat but found no relief.

"Yes, who designed your suit?"

"To tell you the truth, I don't even remember."

"Well, it looked incredible on you. Speaking of looking incredible, how do you feel about Dwayne Johnson beating you out for People Magazine's Sexiest Man Alive this year?"

"I don't really have an opinion about that," Eli was losing patience for the reporter's questions, and really just wanted to stretch his legs.

"You know what, why don't you ask my band here, what they think about it? Excuse me." Eli gently pushed his chair back and dismissed himself with a nod.

"But, we just started…" the reporter's voice trailed off in disbelief, but Eli barely registered her disappointment as he made his way to the elevator. He'd even managed to evade his security guard, who must have been using the bathroom.

Get me the hell out of here. I'm so tired of this shit.

The elevator beeped as the doors opened and Eli stepped in. His eyes scanned the floor numbers…B, he pushed. Basement. Moments later, he made his way out of the elevator and looked about. Kitchen staff members for the restaurant above were bustling every which way.

Eli tapped one of them on the shoulder who looked about his size.

"Excuse me, sir. I hate to trouble you, but would you mind lending me your outfit? Here, you can have mine," Eli was already taking off his jacket.

"Wait, you're that rock star guy, aren't you?" The staff member before him asked. "Way cool. Sure, dude." The man took off his white coat and pants and traded with Eli.

"Much appreciated," Eli quickly put the outfit on top of his underclothes. "I need the hat, too."

"Here, take it."

Eli placed the white cap atop his head. "Excellent, now could you show me the way out of here? Utility entrance, please." He was escorted through an open garage door, after which he quickly turned a corner and began a concerted stroll down the street.

He must have looked foolish, but he didn't care. He was a free man. He had successfully evaded the entourage.

I'm going to go for a walk, he decided. It might loosen the knot in my back.

Eli turned another corner and careened up Bush Street. His cell phone was ringing, but he wasn't going to answer it. Mute. This is my time. It's my fucking birthday.

He hadn't gone more than half a block before a piece of music caught his ear. Sitar. Eli recognized the instrument. It was a Hindustani classical piece. Beautiful. Where was it coming from? Eli traced the sound to a doorway just ahead. He stood there, transfixed. He closed his eyes and delighted in the sound and the calm that overtook his body as he listened.

Eli was oblivious to the traffic and street noise around him. In his mind, he felt transported to a temple he had once visited in India. His band had done a photo shoot there a few years before. He had felt something then, too, from merely the walls themselves. Some sort of…energetic communication of…truth? The thought made him feel foolish. Well, he hadn't had time to explore what he'd felt. It was surely nothing. In fact, he'd forgotten about that experience until now.

"Are you just going to stand there, or are you going to come in?"

Eli was shaken out of his trance. He opened his eyes and saw a woman standing before him. She appeared to be of Indian descent, though her American accent told him she must have been raised in the U.S. Eli couldn't help but notice her beauty; he was captivated. She had a slender, but muscular build; he could see it outlined clearly, in her yoga pants and a tank top. Her skin was dark olive, and her long, black hair was pulled back into a ponytail. Her eyes were what killed him. They were the color of coffee, laced with sweetness.

He felt an instant attraction, but it wasn't so much sexual as it was…spiritual? Her enigmatic energy couldn't be denied. What the fuck? He felt like he'd been whipped. Where were his words?

"We have a beginner yoga class starting in just a few minutes. Would you like to join us?"

Eli managed to piece together a sentence, "Um. I don't suppose I'm…properly dressed."

She laughed, "Your…attire will do just fine. It's loose fitting, and that's all that matters."

"Hmm. Well, I've never done it before."

"No problem. I will guide you. You must come in now

though. I have to lock the door and begin; the students are waiting. There's no cost if you're worried about that."

He hadn't worried about the cost of anything in years. It felt refreshing, however, to clearly not be recognized.

"It might help get that kink out of your back," she winked.

How did she know my back hurts? Eli thought, confused. Maybe she saw me wince or something. Anyway, she does have a point…what do I have to lose? "Ok, I will try it."

"Good. Glad that's settled," she smiled.

Eli stepped inside the yoga studio. The lights were drawn dim, and a small table at the front of the room displayed a statue of a goddess, surrounded by candles. Tapestries hung along the walls, of every color imaginable and detailed design. Eli noticed the Fibonacci sequence everywhere.

"Here's a mat you can borrow. And a block. You might need it," the woman handed him a thin blue mat and a purple foam block.

"My name is Angelina. I will be your teacher."

Eli smiled. Angelina.

"And what is your name?"

"Oh, I'm sorry. My name is… Elijah." He didn't want to blow his cover.

"Welcome, Elijah. Please have a seat at the top of your mat. We will begin."

CHAPTER SEVEN

──────⟨⟨⟨∞⟩⟩⟩──────

ANGELINA

E li ambled awkwardly to a spot in the back of the room, where he set down the block and rolled out the mat Angelina had handed him. He took his cue from the other six students in the room and sat cross-legged at the top of the mat, facing the altar. This position alone felt like a struggle. *What have I gotten myself into?* Eli thought skeptically.

His body was naturally slender and muscular, a result of all of the physical labor he'd engaged in on the farm over the years, and he had a personal trainer with whom he lifted weights, but Eli couldn't remember the last time he'd stretched.

Angelina dimmed the lights and lowered the music slightly before taking her position at the head of the room.

"Good afternoon, yogis," she spoke softly, her words preceded and followed by a deep, conscious breath.

Yogi? Eli laughed to himself. *Hardly.* If it weren't for the burgeoning pain he felt in his back and Angelina's alluring presence, he might have curtailed it out of there right then. Clearly, he thought, he was not one of "them." But he wasn't about to display any such weakness in front of this woman he was already becoming infatuated with.

"Welcome to class. This is a beginning Iyengar class. Some of you I have seen here before, but there are a couple of new faces today." Angelina nodded in Eli's direction and he felt his heart beat faster.

"For those of you new to the class, this is a style of yoga that focuses heavily on detail. It can be easy to injure one's self when just starting out in the practice if the alignment of the body is not properly paid attention to. As we move through the various *asanas*, or poses, in class today, I want you to focus less on speed or how deep you can stretch, and more on breath and precision. I will give highly-detailed verbal instruction as I walk around and correct any misalignment or unnecessary tension I recognize in your bodies. Now, does anyone here have any objection to physical contact?"

Eli looked around the room; there was only one other male, a gray-haired gentleman with a bit of a belly who appeared to be in his late fifties. He couldn't imagine he'd have any objection. Eli certainly did not. No one raised a hand.

"Great. Now, I'd like each of you to set an intention for this class. As you consider what that might be, let me share a bit about the philosophy of Iyengar yoga. As humans in modern society, so much of our energy is focused on that which is external—what we see, hear, feel, and experience outside of ourselves. Many of us spend our days rushing from one activity or place to the next, giving very little thought or attention to what is going on inside of ourselves. The goal of this practice is to increase our awareness of our emotional, physical, and spiritual lives. Strive to leave no part of yourself neglected or undiscovered."

Eli had known for some time now that he hadn't been paying enough attention to any of those aspects of his life—

his career allowed little time for personal exploration. *Well, I'm here now,* he granted himself.

"Now, think about your intention. For example, maybe it's to give yourself a ninety-minute reprieve from external stimulation. Perhaps it's to prepare yourself emotionally for a tough conversation you have to have with a loved one. Maybe it's to heal a physical part of yourself that has been neglected or in pain. I'll give you a few moments to settle your thoughts."

My intention is to gather the courage to ask that girl out. It was superficial, Eli admitted. But not entirely. She made him feel something he hadn't felt for quite some time... many things, actually. For one, he didn't feel like a rock star; he felt like Eli. Second, he already felt more present. There was something about her voice; it had a melodic tone that instantly calmed him.

"Alright. Let's hold our intention in our hearts and sound three rounds of *om* together." *Now, this I can handle,* Eli thought. His music teacher in grade school had made him chant *om* more times than he could count. It was a comforting resonance he'd nearly forgotten he always had at his disposal.

"*Ommmmm....*" Angelina began, and the class joined in. Eli couldn't help but notice the hesitation the other students felt towards letting their voices be heard. Naturally, Eli held no self-consciousness in that respect. His beautiful baritone filled the room, causing Angelina to open her eyes slightly in order to discern its source.

At the conclusion of the three rounds, Angelina seemed as though she had to regain her composure slightly. The class waited for her to speak.

"Okay, let's begin our physical practice with downward-facing dog." Angelina demonstrated the pose as she described it. "Firmly place your hands and walk your feet back. As you straighten the arms out, rotate them out. Focus on lengthening the sides of the chest as you push your buttocks up and push your thighbones back to take the heels down. Push your hips back to root your heels down further. That's it."

Angelina stood and began walking about the room. "Be careful not to let your chest sink down," she corrected a young female student in the front of the room. "Relax the neck, Robert," she continued around the room until reaching Eli. Already, he was shaking. "Try bending your knees, Elijah. Does that help?" He did as she said, but felt little relief in his lower back. She sensed his discomfort. "Let's come down slowly now. Relax into child's pose for a few moments."

"How is that?"

"Come to your knees, sit back on your heels, and stretch your arms out in front of you. You can lean your forehead on the ground, there." Angelina lightly placed her hands on Eli's back. One hand remained stabilized near his sacrum as she stretched her other hand upwards along his spine, ever so slowly. "How does that feel?"

Eli couldn't find the words to describe how it felt. He'd never felt anything like it. His body was no longer shaking, it was *vibrating*—internally. Energy had passed through him like a bolt of electricity. *I knew I was attracted to the girl, but what the fuck was that? That was a whole other level*, he thought in bewilderment.

"It feels...good," was all he managed.

"Are you feeling any pain?"

Hmm. Surprisingly, his back did feel better. "Not really."

"Good. Try getting into downward-dog again. Class, the rest of you can come down into child's pose now."

Eli stretched his legs back again and reached his arms out. "Spread your fingers wide," he was instructed. "Good. That looks much better. Your legs aren't shaking anymore."

And they weren't. But he did notice his heart was beating faster.

CLASS ENSUED WITH A SERIES OF GENTLE POSES. ELI SURPRISED himself that he was able to keep up with the other students, all of whom had attended at least a few classes before. He was not very flexible, that was for sure, but he realized that he did not lack strength when he went into what Angelina had called *Chaturanga*. *My hamstrings will feel the class tomorrow*, he thought, but really, he was more focused on today.

After a short rest in "corpse pose," or *savasana*, Angelina asked the class to sit back up.

"Please place your palms together and hold them against your chest. Now, remember the intention you set for the class. Isn't it beautiful that we always have the opportunity to be a higher version of who we are with each new moment? *Namaste.*"

"*Namaste,*" the class repeated, bowing their heads momentarily before rising and rolling up their mats.

Now, about that intention, Eli thought. Why was he so nervous? He'd been with more beautiful women than he could count. *But they threw themselves at me*, Eli considered. *I didn't have to do a damn thing.* This time, there was a chance of rejection—an experience Eli hadn't feared in many years. Suddenly, he felt like Eli the boy again. That awareness in equal parts scared him and delighted him.

He waited until the remaining five students left the room. He lingered casually near the door, taking longer than he needed to put his shoes back on.

"Is your back feeling better? It was awful tight."

"Hmm? Oh, yes. I did something to it on—" Eli caught himself, "On a walk the other day." *On a walk?*

"There are many possible causes for lower back pain. But often it is the result of emotions that have been left ignored."

"How so?"

"Well, the psoas muscle, which is the muscle that moves your hip joints, is supported by kidney energy flow. Chronic fear and anxiety restrict the necessary flow of energy from the kidney to your psoas muscle, making you more susceptible to lower back pain. Do you have a stressful job, perhaps?"

Eli had to contain a laugh. "Somewhat stressful, yes."

"Our bodies give us signals all the time. Pain is a useful tool; it serves as a message that something is off balance in our lives. It could be our diet or another aspect of our physical behavior, or sometimes it's emotional. Humans don't like to look at pain; we do everything in our power to make it go away—taking pills, ignoring it…but we have to look it in the face if we ever hope to overcome it."

"Did you study anatomy and physiology or something?"

"Well, not academically. I've learned a lot through my yoga practice. And through growing up in an ashram."

"You grew up in an ashram?"

Angelina laughed, "Yes. Everyone seems so shocked by that."

"No, I guess I'm not shocked. I mean, you have a very… strong energy about you. It makes sense."

"Well, anyway, I left the society when I turned eighteen. It's a long story. I don't want to bore you with it."

"It's not boring at all. I'd love to hear it."

"Maybe sometime. If you come to another class," Angelina winked. "Now I have to prepare for my level three class." The first student was already entering the studio.

"Welcome, Sarah."

"Hi, Angelina!"

Eli fought the urge to scowl at Sarah for interrupting his moment. "Hey, listen, Angelina…could we…continue this conversation later? Would you be interested in joining me for a drink this evening? Or…I don't know…a kombucha? Is that what 'yogis' drink?" he smiled playfully.

"I can't tonight," she sounded regretful, but Eli's heart sank.

"I'll tell you what though. Here's my number," she reached for a business card. "I'm free this weekend."

This weekend. Eli wasn't even sure what state he would be in four days later. Never mind. He had a number.

"I'll call you," he smiled.

"I'll look forward to it," she grinned back.

Eli gathered his jacket and reached for the door.

"Oh, Elijah?"

"Yes?"

"You have a beautiful voice."

It was certainly not the first time Eli had been told such words but never had they sounded any sweeter.

Eli left the studio with a wide grin on his face. His reverie was interrupted, however, when he remembered his band. It had been nearly two hours since he'd left them in the press interview. He took out his phone and regrettably turned it back on. *Fifteen voicemails. Jesus Christ.* He wasn't going to listen to them. He knew what they'd say. Instead, he called his manager.

"Eli! What the hell, man? Where have you been? Everyone's been worried sick about you! Are you okay?"

"I was at a…never mind, man. I'm fine. Never been better, actually."

"Okay…" Eli got the sense his manager didn't want to know. "Well, where are you? We're all still at the magazine's building. We didn't know if you were coming back or what. We'll come pick you up."

"Never mind, no need. I'm just around the corner. I'll meet you in the lobby in a few minutes."

"No, don't go to the lobby. The crowd is still there. We'll come to you."

"Okay, just a minute," Eli glanced around, looking for a quieter street. He sure as hell didn't want to be picked up in front of the yoga studio. "There's an alley. Harlan Place. Meet me at the end of that street. Look for the chef's suit."

"What? Whatever. We'll be there in a few."

"Oh, wait. Russ?"

"Yeah?"

"Where are we playing this weekend?"

"This weekend? Friday night Denver, Saturday Salt Lake, Sunday Boise."

Shit.

"No wait, Boise isn't until Monday. Sunday we're off."

Oh, hell yeah.

"Great, okay thanks. See you soon."

"Yep."

The limo arrived shortly. After several minutes of being teased by his bandmates for his outfit, his drummer, Richard, turned to him with genuine concern. "Seriously, man, are you really okay? I mean, you look much better, but you scared us all there."

"Yeah, yeah, sorry guys. I won't do that again. Let's grab some dinner, what do you say? We've got time before rehearsal."

"Burgers and Barbeque?"

Eli shrugged his shoulders, "Yes, of course." *This birthday is shaping up to be pretty damn good*, he thought.

ELI DIDN'T GET A CHANCE TO CALL ANGELINA UNTIL SATURDAY afternoon. He hadn't wanted to make the call in front of the guys. He wasn't ready to share with anyone that he'd met someone he was deeply interested in. *Word spreads like wildfire when you're famous*, he thought.

He called her from his hotel room in Salt Lake City. He was insanely nervous, once again. *How can I play nightly to crowds in the thousands and not have a single butterfly, but when I want to call just one woman, I nearly lose it?*

Dialing her number slowly, he did what he knew she'd tell him to do if she were there—he took a deep breath.

"Hello?" she answered on the fourth ring.

"Hi, hello. Is this Angelina?"

"Yes."

"This is Eli..jah. From the yoga class the other day."

"Elijah. I was beginning to think you weren't going to call."

"Oh, sorry. I've been traveling. Hey, so, I'd really like to take you out for that drink…or actually, dinner if you're up for it. Are you free tomorrow night?"

"I am."

"Great. Dinner then?"

"I would like that."

"You pick the place."

"Is vegetarian okay?"

Eli chuckled. A far cry from what he was used to on the road. "Yes, absolutely."

"How about Holy Kitchen? It's in Noe Valley—it's an Indian restaurant."

"Perfect. Six p.m.? I'll pick you up?"

"Just meet me there."

"As you wish," Eli was actually relieved—he wouldn't have to explain why he arrived in a rental car.

"I'll see you tomorrow night then."

"Tomorrow night," Eli could hear the smile in her voice. He was overjoyed at the thought that she genuinely seemed to like him. *And she doesn't even know who I am.*

ELI ARRANGED FOR A PRIVATE CHARTER FLIGHT FROM SALT Lake City to San Francisco the following afternoon. He told his manager he had a cousin there he wanted to visit and he'd spend the night with him. "I'll see you in Boise by early Monday afternoon," he promised. He rarely traveled alone, but his manager was getting used to Eli's erratic behavior as of late; he hadn't shown any interest in the string of women he'd been introduced to at shows the past few nights, and he could have sworn he heard him chanting in his hotel room the night before.

He arrived in San Francisco at 3:00 in the afternoon. He'd arranged for a Toyota Corolla to await him at the airport; he preferred to blend in rather than impress. However, he did splurge on a hotel room at The St. Regis, as he'd become quite accustomed to luxury accommodations. He had no intention of letting Angelina in on the fact, quite yet, that he didn't live in San Francisco, so inviting her back to the hotel was out of the question.

After settling into his Presidential suite, Eli decided to take advantage of the hotel's spa services; he wanted to be as relaxed and present as possible for his evening plans. He indulged in the saltwater pool followed by a short cleanse in the sauna. He hadn't soaked or used a sauna in several months, and this dedicated time for himself felt like a guilty pleasure. He returned to his room feeling rejuvenated from the last few nights on the road.

Eli had packed light; he brought a black, button-down Lewis and Taylor dress shirt, and a pair of rustic J. Crew jeans, which he changed into after a short nap and a shave. *I still look like a rock star*, Eli thought begrudgingly while looking at himself in the mirror. *Perhaps it's time to let the long hair go.* Eli's PR rep had recommended he maintain his shoulder-length locks in order to emphasize a youthful and rugged image. "The ladies love it, Eli." She had told him to keep his bangs long, loosely hanging over his eyes to add an element of "mystery."

His hairstyle had, in fact, become somewhat iconic; he noticed more fans in the audience cutting their hair in a similar fashion than he ever had before. *But what about what I want?* he thought. It was annoying to have hair in his eyes all the time. And perhaps he'd be less recognizable with a new haircut—at least until his next show. *Yes, I will cut it*, he decided.

Eli phoned the concierge and arranged to have a prominent Bay area hairstylist come to his room within the hour. "Cut it short, please, with a tapered nape and choppy on top." The result was striking; his hazel eyes shown prominently now, and his chiseled jawbone appeared on display. He felt like a new version of himself—one that was perhaps, more vulnerable. He liked it though. *I hope Angelina likes it, too,* he thought.

Eli grabbed his sunglasses, slid his wallet into his pocket, and notified valet he was ready for his car. After riding the elevator down to the lobby, he asked the receptionist where the flowers on her desk had come from. Perhaps it was a bit old-fashioned, but he wanted to surprise Angelina. "Sir, you are welcome to have these," the receptionist smiled sweetly. "In fact, I insist." Eli hesitated, but he was running short on time. "Thank you kindly," he slid a $100 bill across the counter and walked off with the small bouquet of yellow calla lilies and purple iris hydrangea.

The car's GPS navigation system smoothly directed him to Noe Valley. He was not accustomed to driving much by himself, and he realized now how much he'd missed it. He'd casually scrolled through radio stations and, not surprisingly, heard his latest single, "Breathtaking," within the first fifteen minutes of his drive. He'd changed the station, however—it was easier than fighting his tendency to overanalyze and self-critique what was already in the can.

It took him several minutes to find parking near the restaurant, but he didn't mind. He was early. He waited until exactly 6:00 p.m. before walking through the front door. She was already there—he could see her seated at a table for two in the back of the room.

"Hello! How may I help you?" the hostess greeted him.

"Hi, yes. My party has already arrived, there in the back." She led him to Angelina's table.

Angelina stood, "Elijah! I'm sorry I didn't see you come in. I...didn't recognize you."

"I'm going incognito tonight," Eli smiled. "Nice to see

you," he kissed her cheek in greeting. Her smell was delicious.

"Nice to see you, too. I like your haircut. Very stylish."

"Thank you. You look beautiful." *Radiant would be a better word.* She had the same glow he'd recognized the moment he first saw her. He couldn't decide if she was more beautiful in her yoga clothes or tonight—her black, silky hair left to cascade down her back. She wore turquoise earrings and matching bracelet, a spaghetti-strap orange and red dress perfectly framing her petite body. He nearly lost his breath.

Holding the flowers out to her, he shyly confessed, "I saw these and thought of you."

"They're beautiful, Elijah. Thank you."

"I can place those in a vase and hold them at the counter for you," the hostess offered.

"Yes, please. That would be great," Angelina answered before turning to Eli as the two took their seats. "So. How have you been?"

"Very well, thank you," Eli suddenly felt like he'd forgotten how to talk to women. *I sound like I'm at a press interview or something. Lighten up, Eli.*

"You said you've been traveling. Where did you go?"

"Oh, yes. Salt Lake City," *and Los Angeles and Las Vegas and Denver...*Eli thought but dared not mention.

"Business or pleasure?"

"Business, I suppose."

"You suppose?" Angelina grinned.

"Well, yes. I had a...meeting there."

"I see," Angelina sensed Eli's reluctance to talk about work. "How is your back?"

"Much better. Well, it still hurts sometimes, but not nearly as bad." Cautiously, Eli shared, "You...did something to it."

"In what sense?"

"I…I felt something go through me, actually. When you corrected my pose. It may sound silly, but there was…heat."

"Mmm hmm," Eli caught Angelina trying to suppress a grin.

"What?"

Surrendering to her smile, Angelina replied, "Well, it's just…I practice Reiki. I used an energy healing technique on your lower back."

"Huh." *And here I thought it was just our chemistry,* Eli thought. *Well, it was, in a way.* "So, you practice Reiki. How did you get into that? Oh wait, let me guess. At the ashram?"

Angelina laughed, "No, I actually learned Reiki later."

"Can I get you two started off with something to drink?" the waitress had arrived, bringing the menus. Eli ordered a glass of wine, though he slightly regretted it when Angelina ordered tea.

"Please, tell me more about growing up in an ashram."

"Sure. I was born into the religion of Sikh Dharma. My parents were followers of guru Yogi Bhajan, so I was raised as one, too. The experience was a great gift, in a lot of ways. I don't know that my spiritual development would be where it's at without that experience. It's where I learned meditation, Kundalini yoga, and many other energy awareness practices."

"So why did you leave?"

"As I grew older, the veil over my eyes was lifted, so to speak. I still believe in a lot of the teachings, but I don't agree with many of them—particularly the way women are treated. I left when the guru insisted I move forward with marriage to a partner he had arranged for me. That's when I moved to San Francisco."

"Wow. I'm glad you got out."

"My parents are still followers. They wear turbans and live in a Sikh community in Los Angeles, where I was raised. They were an arranged marriage themselves. My mother is from America, and my father is Indian."

"Are they happily married? Sorry, that's probably rude of me to ask. I've never known anyone in an arranged marriage before."

"No, it's okay. In a sense; my mother is content with her role. My father…he travels a lot, which is probably why my mother doesn't mind the marriage," Angelina joked, but she knew there was truth behind her words.

"Are you two ready to order?" the waitress had returned with their drinks.

"I am. I'd like the chana masala, please. With a side of naan bread." Angelina stated. Turning to Eli she confessed, "I always get the same thing."

"And for you, Sir?"

"Um, yes. I'll have the same. Thank you." He didn't know what most of the items on the menu were.

"I'm doing all the talking. What about you, Eli? Where did you grow up?"

"Brownsville, Oregon. On a farm."

She laughed, "No way! You look nothing like a farm boy."

"It's true. Population 1,693."

"Well, I never would have guessed that. What was that like?"

"I suppose, like your experience, it was a blessing in a lot of ways. Most kids grow up in concrete cities with manu-factured playgrounds. For me, the creek, the fields and the hills were my playground. My surroundings cultivated the imagination to a much greater extent. I was raised deeply connected to nature."

"Sounds amazing."

"Yeah. You know, it really was," Eli reflected. "But I couldn't wait to get out, too. I left before finishing high school."

"Oh, wow. Why so soon?"

"An opportunity to travel the world was presented to me. And I have, that's for sure. But at some point…every place starts to seem the same." Eli's thoughts trailed off momentarily. "Sometimes I really miss the farm. The simplicity of it all. The peace…the privacy."

Angelina allowed him the space for silence. They were interrupted within moments, however. "Two chana masalas. Enjoy."

Eli appeared slightly startled. He mumbled a delayed, "Thank you," after the waitress had already turned away.

"Is everything alright?" Angelina questioned.

"Hmm? Yes. Sometimes I just wonder what the purpose of it all is, you know?"

"The purpose of what in particular?"

"Life. We're always trying to reach the top, of whatever it is—the corporate ladder, the music charts…the mountaintop. But what then? What happens when you're there, and you still feel like something's missing?"

"That's when you go within," Angelina answered quietly but confidently. "There's much more to explore inside of ourselves than outside."

"Yeah, but when does one find the time to do that? Amid all of our 'worldly responsibilities,' you know?"

"When you want something bad enough, you make the time. And the beautiful thing is, you can do it from anywhere.

People think meditation is so hard—that there are all these rules: you have to practice in an ashram or a special studio, you have to be dressed a certain way or in a perfectly quiet environment. It's not like that.

"Just close your eyes—if you even want to do that—anytime, anywhere, and listen. Redirect your thoughts when they come up, without judging them when they do, to the present. You can focus on a blade of grass even, or the quietest sound you can hear. Guidance will come to you. You'll discover things about yourself, simply because you're open to hearing them."

Eli went silent again, but his gaze was intent on Angelina.

"Sorry. I get excited about this topic. I'm talking too much."

Eli took a deep breath in and slowly let it out before whispering, "I love it."

THE REMAINDER OF THEIR DINNER WAS SPENT IN COMFORTable silence. Neither of them felt they had to fill a void. Eli couldn't remember the last time he'd been so aware of his surroundings—probably not since he was a boy on the farm. He was putting Angelina's suggestion into practice, listening to the clank of the silverware, his own light breathing.

He heard the subtle buzz of the light fixtures above them, and he believed he'd also picked up on Angelina's growing affection for him. It was different than the kind he was used to from women; this was more…tender.

As they stood to leave the restaurant, Eli placed his hand on the small of her back and gently guided her to the door. "Don't forget your flowers," he winked.

"I wasn't about to," she smiled back at him.

The two made their way to the street. "Can I offer you a ride home? Or…anywhere?"

"That won't be necessary. My apartment is only a twenty-minute walk from here, in the Mission."

"May I walk you home?"

"I'd like that very much."

Eli reached for her hand, "My lady."

Angelina laughed and took his hand. Once again, Eli felt a wave of energy flow from her hand and up his arm. *I don't think* that *is because of Reiki*, he thought. *Did she feel that too?* he wondered. He decided to take his chances. With his empty hand, he reached up and gently held her face as he bent down and softly kissed her lips.

Angelina kissed back. *Thank you, God*, Eli thought to himself. Her lips were saccharine. As he pulled back slowly and looked into her eyes, he felt *seen*—like he hadn't truly been seen in a long time. *Somehow, she knows me*, he pondered. Angelina, meanwhile, reflected. *where have I seen him before?*

She was caught off guard by her gravitation toward him; there were so few men she'd deemed worthy of dating. But she wanted to know this man better.

The two continued, hand in hand, the fifteen blocks to Angelina's apartment. Eli made no assumption that he'd be invited to enter, but he hoped with all his might that their time together that night was not about to end.

"Here we are," she paused in front of a sunlight yellow Victorian flat with gingerbread trim. "Would you like to see inside?"

Would he ever. "I'd love to."

Angelina smiled in response. She unlocked the door and led the way inside her studio apartment. Eli felt like he was in Europe, or perhaps India. Plants hung from the ceiling, sat in pots in corners and on counter spaces near windows.

Goddess statues, decorated with colorful beads and jewelry, seemed to extend invitations to sit before them. Colorful tapestries hung as section dividers. The only furniture was a futon that was laid out as a bed, and an array of pillows that sat around a low table.

"It's beautiful," Eli remarked.

"Thank you. It's small, but it's all I need."

Eli stood awkwardly; he did not want to sit on her bed without being invited.

"Would you like some tea? Or, I think you might prefer wine?"

"I'll have some tea," oddly, tea did sound preferable to him, though it was something he had only ever drunk when coffee wasn't available.

"Is chamomile alright?"

"Sure."

Angelina moved to the kitchen area and put on the kettle.

"Take a seat. Please, make yourself comfortable." She gestured to the pillows around the table. Eli accepted her cue and sat upon an Indian floor cushion.

Eli had grown to feel claustrophobic in small spaces—perhaps it was due to all the time he'd spent on the bus. But here, at Angelina's, the studio space felt comforting. Safe.

"Do you mind if I put on some music?"

"Not at all."

The ambient sound of sitar offered pleasant, light background music. It was the same music Eli had first heard playing at Angelina's studio. He wondered if that was intentional.

"Who is playing?"

"Ravi Shankar. And George Harrison."

"George Harrison the rock star?" Eli chucked.

"Yes, the Beatle. The album is called Collaborations. Shankar was traditionally a performer of Hindustani classical ragas, but this album dives into jazz and rock and Indian folk. I love it."

Eli was aware of the album, but he didn't want to mention it.

"What kind of music do you like?"

Eli held back a smile at the question. "Oh, a little of everything, really. But if I had to pick a favorite overarching genre, it would be blues. What about you?"

"I mostly listen to traditional Indian folk music, to be honest. I don't like contemporary music all that much. It feels too…programmed."

Eli laughed, "Yeah a lot of it can be."

The tea kettle whistled and Angelina poured two cups, then brought them to the table.

"Careful, it's hot."

Eli winced suddenly.

"What is it? What's wrong?"

"It's nothing, I just felt another spasm in my back. It happens occasionally."

"I can help you with that. Please, if you will, lie down on the futon."

Eli would have been boyishly eager to jump to her bed, had the pain not kept him from making sudden movements. He rose slowly, his hand upon his back, and carefully sat on the edge of the futon. Angelina helped move his legs over to the side and instructed him to turn over onto his stomach.

She rubbed her hands together quickly, garnering some heat, before placing them lightly on his sacrum. She began breathing deeply; Eli could feel the subtle release of Angelina's breath upon his neck. After what felt like several minutes, the heat from her hands had become so strong, he could feel it spread along his spine and extend all the way through his fingertips and toes. His whole body tingled.

"What is that? What am I feeling?"

"It's your chi—your life force. That's good that you feel it. Energy that has been stuck is moving."

Angelina noticed Eli's breath start to slow. "How does your back feel now?"

"Better. Relaxed. Thank you." Eli was grateful for the relief. Flipping over onto his back, he looked up at Angelina, who was still seated beside him. She held his gaze in a moment of shared gratitude.

"I am happy to be of help."

"Tell me more about chi. I'd like to learn about it."

"Okay. Well, the human body has seven chakras, or energy centers. When energy in one or more of the chakras gets blocked, illness or disease can occur there. Your pain is in your root chakra—at the base of your spine in the tailbone area. This is the chakra that is associated with your foundation, or the feeling of being grounded."

"What are the other chakras?"

"The sacral chakra—right here—Angelina placed her hand lightly on Eli's lower abdomen, "represents our ability to accept others and new experiences. The solar plexus chakra," Angelina shifted her hand to Eli's upper abdomen, "represents our ability to be confident and in control of our lives.

"The heart chakra," Angelina placed her hand at the center of Eli's chest, just above his heart, "is the chakra representing love, joy, and inner peace."

The top two buttons of Eli's shirt were unbuttoned, allowing him to feel Angelina's hand in direct contact with his skin. He could hardly take it. His heart beat faster; he was certain Angelina must have felt it. He wondered if her heart was racing, too.

"May I feel yours?" It felt like a bold question, but he was feeling more courageous.

To his surprise, she nodded in acquiescence. Eli placed his hand in the center of her chest. He melted at the slight touch of her breasts but tried to focus on her heartbeat. *It's beating quickly.* He held her gaze for a few moments before slowly sitting up. For the second time that night, he held her face in his hands and brought his lips to hers.

This time, the kiss was infused with passion. After a minute, Angelina leaned her forehead against his, maintaining intimate contact but gently pulling her lips back from his. "Slowly," she whispered. "Breathe."

Eli's breath was heavy.

"With me. Match mine. It's a dance."

Eli placed his hand back near her heart and listened for her breath. Joining her rhythm, he pulled his face back slightly in order to look her in the eyes.

"That's better," she smiled.

Eli's jeans had become tight; he wanted to unbutton them and release the pressure, but he dared not move. Angelina had not let go of his gaze, and he sensed he should not be the first to do so.

Finally, after what felt like an eternity, she reached across and further unbuttoned his shirt. She placed one hand on either side of his shoulders underneath his shirt, and let his shirt fall behind him. She gestured that it was alright for him to undress her.

Eli slipped two fingers beneath one strap of her dress and gently encouraged it to fall. One breast was revealed; she had not worn a bra. Eli was infatuated with its beauty. It was perfectly round and firm, her nipple was alive and inviting. He wanted nothing more than to reach his lips to it, but he could sense it wasn't the right time.

Reaching his hand to the other strap of her dress, he let it fall to her waist. A gorgeous display of feminine power sat before him. Her body was molded with an exquisite balance between muscle and softness.

Angelina allowed him to take her upper body in for several moments before she stood and took his hand, leading him to stand beside her. As she stood, her dress slipped off her waist, revealing her long, toned legs. *Dear God,* he thought.

She reached across and finally undid his pants, ever so slowly. Reaching her hands behind him, she placed them down his pants and let her hands glaze his backside before drawing his pants down to the floor with her thumbs. Only their underwear remained. Angelina stepped forward and pressed her body up against his, holding him in a tight embrace.

"Your breath," she reminded him. He had forgotten. This time, he felt her heartbeat with his chest. He waited for his own chest to rise and fall with hers. It was a level of intimacy he had rarely—if ever—experienced with a woman. Suddenly, he became aware of what had been missing in his life. *Connection.* Heart-centered, soul-awakening connection. He'd never opened himself up to feel so much. He felt as though he might cry. *What is happening?* Taken aback by the flood of emotions he had undergone, Eli felt fear return to his state of mind. *What does this mean?*

All of the women he'd slept with—all of the relationships he'd had over the years, of both the sexual and non-sexual variety—were any of them real? Even his family—had he ever truly known them in this way? *I once did.* Eli recalled an early childhood memory of being seated on the couch with his mother. He'd jumped into her lap and laid his head on her chest. He'd recognized her heartbeat; it was the most comforting sensation he'd ever felt. Love…he'd felt so deeply loved. And he'd been aware, even then, that it was mutual.

"I love you, Mama," he'd said, as he kissed her cheek.

"Are you ok?" Angelina's voice shook him away from his memory.

"Yes, I am. Are you ok?"

"I am."

Angelina. This beautiful woman before him. He wanted her now more than any moment before. This time, Angelina allowed him to kiss her fervidly. Eli reached a hand to her panties and slowly brought them to the floor. He swept his arms around her back and legs and lifted her up, carrying her to the kitchen counter. Eli registered her surprise, but she did not resist.

He took her in with his eyes before tracing her vulva with the same two fingers he'd used to remove her dress straps. *Like a flower,* he thought. She was moist. He couldn't wait to enter her. He dropped his own underwear to the floor, his penis large and erect before her. Eli moved slowly, but assuredly, running his fingers through her hair as his penis found her body's entrance. Lightning went off in his mind. *So, warm, so soft.*

Angelina's head tilted back as her back arched slightly. Sweat had formed on her neckline, and Eli swept his tongue along it. Her body pulsated at the touch of his tongue. Eli made his penis dance inside of her, in and out, in and out slowly and gently. Angelina leaned forward, locking her legs around his waist and her arms around his neck. She kissed his neck before lowering one hand to guide Eli's hand down from her breast to her sacrum.

From that place deep within her, Angelina let out a moan that caused Eli to not be able to contain himself any longer. He came inside of her, the most rewarding release he'd ever felt. Angela felt deep pleasure too, but also entertained the thought, *He's not yet ready. But he's teachable.*

THEY SPENT THE NIGHT ON THE FUTON IN A LIGHT EMBRACE. Eli couldn't remember a time he'd slept so deeply. He awoke abruptly, however, to the sound of an alarm. "What the?" Eli squinted his eyes; a glance at the clock on the wall told him it was only 5:30 a.m.

Angelina reached across his body to quiet the alarm then leaned above him, smiling as she kissed his forehead. "I teach a sunrise yoga class." Eli let his head fall back onto the pillow, as he covered his eyes with his arm. "For real?"

"Yep," Angelina grinned. "You are welcome to stay in bed if you like. Just lock the door before you leave. There's some cold tea on the table you can have for breakfast," she joked. "No, seriously. Help yourself to anything you find."

Eli considered getting up, but his body did not move. "What time will you be back?"

"I have classes all day. You can come later if you want. My beginner yoga class is at 3:00 p.m. You might remember."

"Right, 3:00." *Shit*, Eli remembered his commitments for the day. "I can't. I'm sorry. I'd love to, but I have a flight to catch. I have a…meeting in Boise this afternoon."

"In Boise? You do travel a lot."

"Yes. It's part of my job."

"You still haven't told me what kind of work you do."

"I'll tell you…on our next date," Eli smiled mischievously.

"Deal," Angelina grinned as she stepped into the shower. "Now go back to sleep."

Eli yawned, "Ok. I'll call you from Boise," he mumbled as he flipped over onto his back. He had a few hours yet, he figured, before he'd need to return to the hotel. *And my rock star life*, he thought as he fell back asleep.

Petra Nicoll

CHAPTER EIGHT

A GREAT TEACHER

For a moment, Eli forgot where he was. The night before had felt like a dream, and his conversation with Angelina that morning had barely registered. As he began to recover his senses, he pleasurably recalled the experience he just had with the woman he had not been able to stop thinking about over the past several days.

His delight was challenged, however, by his disappointment—and disbelief—that she had left him there, in her apartment. *At least she trusts me*, he thought. He had never been left like that after a night of intimacy before; it was always he that unemotionally shared the news, "I have to go. Have a nice day."

Despite the slight bruise to his ego, he was encouraged by the fact that Angelina was an independent woman—which only added to her allure. He had to get ready to catch his flight to Boise, anyway. Eli stood, stretched, and gathered his things before taking one quick glance around her apartment. He noticed, for the first time, a headshot of Angelina that hung on her refrigerator. In black marker, the words "Best Actress" were delicately scrawled in what he assumed was Angelina's handwriting.

Hmm. I thought she was just a yoga teacher. Eli considered there was so much more to Angelina he didn't yet know—and of course, hadn't thought to ask. Suddenly, he felt like he was eavesdropping on her life. Preferring to learn more through her own words, he decided to leave her apartment without looking around further. Eli dressed in his clothes from the night before, grabbed his jacket and made his way out the door, locking it behind him.

IT WASN'T AS HARD AS ELI THOUGHT TO FALL BACK INTO HIS regular lifestyle. He'd had time to pleasantly reflect on his time with Angelina while enflight to Boise, but as soon as the flight landed he went back into go-mode. He was picked up by a driver from the venue and led backstage, where he met up with the members of his band. They were curious about where he'd been but were left little time to ask him about it. They moved from sound check to dinner to watching the opening band from backstage before taking the stage themselves.

At the time his performance ended, Eli's thoughts were not even remotely on the night before. He had to step into a rather typical post-show routine: greet and get his picture taken with fan club members, have a short meeting and photo-op with a teenager from the Make a Wish Foundation, either avoid or engage with groupies depending on his mood, have drinks with the band before checking into a hotel or hitting the road towards the next gig.

Tonight, he chose to avoid the groupies and return directly to the bus so they could hit the road early for the next night's gig in Spokane. Enough memory of the night before lingered for him to lack interest in meaningless sex. *I forgot, I told Angelina I'd call her from Boise,* he remembered. It was 1 a.m.

Mountain Time…*Well, that's only midnight in San Francisco,* he considered. Then he remembered she likely had what she'd called a "sunrise" yoga class to teach in the morning. *Damn.* But he had promised…*It's worth a try,* he decided.

Eli slid into his bunk, pulled the curtain for some privacy, and dialed her number from the phone on the wall. After five rings, her voicemail message came on. He thought about leaving a message but realized he had no idea what to say. He didn't even know his schedule for the remainder of the week. He knew they'd be making their way down the West Coast, and he did believe the band had a gig in San Francisco lined up sometime over the next couple of weeks, but he had no idea when.

He could tell her he'd try calling her again tomorrow… but he was pretty certain she'd be in classes all day, and he had another gig to prepare for by the following afternoon. *Hey, I had a great time last night,* he thought about saying, but that sounded too cheesy. Eli knew the beep was coming soon to begin recording, and his thoughts were too confused for him to feel prepared. Eli hung up quickly. *I'll try again sometime soon,* he thought, before joining his bandmates for a game of poker.

THE FOLLOWING FEW DAYS FLEW BY; ELI PLAYED SPOKANE, Vancouver, B.C., and Seattle before he had a moment to himself to consider calling Angelina again. He was in Portland now, and he knew he'd be playing San Francisco that weekend.

A predictable sense of nostalgia had flowed through Eli as the bus arrived in Oregon that afternoon. His parents would not be seeing him play on this leg of the tour, which was just as well since he wouldn't have much time to visit with them before the bus rolled away anyway.

Being near where his family was had him feeling sentimental, regardless. He felt guilty for having let so much time pass before calling Angelina again. He was busy, for certain, but the fact that he knew he'd need to surrender his anonymity by telling her about his fame and lifestyle soon kept him from wanting to make the call.

It's now or never, he decided. With conviction, Eli made his way to a secluded spot in the parking lot behind the venue the band would be playing that night and dialed Angelina's number. On the second ring, he felt an overwhelming sense of comfort at the sound of her voice, "Hello?"

"Hi, Angelina. It's Eli—err, Elijah."

"Yes. I know. I recognized your number."

"Oh. Well, how are you?"

"I'm good. Just finished with classes."

"Are you okay? You sound upset or something?"

"Not upset. Just confused. I thought you'd call sooner."

"I did. I called you the night we saw each other last," Eli tried to cover his guilt with defense.

"I didn't receive a call, Eli. Not then, and not any day in the past week."

Oh, shit. Eli realized he had made the call from the bus phone line, which had a Los Angeles area code. "Oh, Angelina, I'm sorry. I did call that night, but it was from a landline phone. And it was late."

Angelina was silent, not sure if she should believe him. The silence was long enough for Eli to take a different approach and own up to his lack of attention.

"But anyway, I am sorry I didn't call again sooner. I've

been traveling a lot. It gets really busy on the…job. Actually, I promised I'd explain more about what I do when I saw you next. I'd like to see you again, Angelina."

Angelina contemplated if she wanted the same. After what felt like an extremely long and uncomfortable silence she replied, "I'd like that," under her breath.

Eli breathed a sigh of relief. "I'll be back in San Francisco this weekend. To be honest, I'll only be there two nights before traveling again. I'll be arriving Saturday morning, and I'd like to spend the whole day with you if you'll give me the pleasure?"

"Let's meet for brunch. Then I'll decide about the rest of the day," Angelina answered confidently.

"Fair enough. I've got to go, but text me a time and location and I'll be there."

"You better," Angelina was firm but had a smile in her voice. Eli took that as a good sign.

"I look forward to seeing you."

"Me too," Angelina agreed as she hung up the phone.

Eli noticed, for the first time, how fast his heart had been racing.

Eli was the one to arrive early for brunch that Saturday. He was nervous in preparation for what he was about to share. He stood from his table as he saw her enter the restaurant.

She was more beautiful than he'd remembered. Eli walked to meet her and embraced her in a tight hug. He kissed her cheek before looking her sincerely in the eye, "Thank you for coming." Angelina gave him a soft smile and nodded. Eli guided her to a table in the corner that was slightly apart from the others in the room.

Just after the two sat down, Angelina demanded, "Look, Eli. No bullshitting. Before we even order, I want to know why you didn't call me sooner. I don't waste my time with men who are not honest and direct with me."

Jeez. She doesn't pull any punches, Eli thought. *Alright, if that's how she wants it.* "I told you I was very busy, and I was—" Eli could see the look of antipathy on her face. "Wait, hear me out. I'm terrified to tell you what I'm about to tell you. I've loved what we've shared. In the short period of time we've spent together, I've felt more like my true self than I can remember in a very, very long time. I'm more comfortable with you than with anyone—even my own family. And I don't want to ruin that."

'Why would being honest ruin that?"

"Because people get ideas in their heads of who they think I am, or should be. I have zero privacy in my life, and that fact is exhausting. Sometimes I forget even who I am, or wonder if I've ever really known." Eli paused before adding, "You've never asked me my last name."

"True. You've never asked me for mine either."

"It's Evans, Angelina. And in fact, my real name isn't Elijah. It's Eli. Just plain Eli." Eli waited to see if that meant anything to her.

Eli Evans. It sounded familiar, Angelina thought, but she couldn't place it.

"I'm a musician," he offered, before singing a line from his most famous song, *Castaway*. Instantly, her face registered recognition, but she sat speechless.

"I don't live in San Francisco. I live in Los Angeles, although I'm practically never there. I am constantly on tour all over the world, and if I'm not touring, I'm recording and writing and being interviewed by every media outlet imaginable. My face is all over the place, my *life* is all over the fucking place, and just the fact that you're sitting with me here now likely means *your* face will be all over the fucking news. Sorry, but you asked me to be honest," Eli took a deep breath and sighed. "Now, do you still want to have brunch with me?"

Eli gazed directly into Angelina's eyes as he watched them drift around the room, then down at the table, before closing slightly and refocusing on his.

"I do," Angeline finally whispered.

"Good. Glad that's out of the way," Eli smiled, relieved.

THE NEXT SEVERAL MINUTES WERE SPENT IN SILENCE. ANGElina was processing what this news all meant for her, and Eli allowed her that space. Finally, she thoughtfully looked up at Eli and spoke.

"You know, there's something I haven't told you about my career, either."

Eli remained silent.

"I'm also an actress. Well, I want to be an actress...I mean, I've had small roles in a few films, but I want to *really* be an actress."

"So, you want to be rich and famous too, eh?" Eli joked.

"Not in the way that most people do. But yes, I want resources and a voice that can be heard by millions."

"What for?"

"To change the world," Angelina winked. "People are falling off their paths...they don't know who they are anymore. I see more people living unconscious lives than ever before. So many have become...zombies. You know?"

"I do know..."

"I want to help lead people back to themselves, and their true purpose in life."

"Well, I can see you being wonderful at that."

"Thank you."

The two finished eating and Eli took care of the bill. As they walked out to the door, he turned to Angelina, "Have I earned more time with you today?"

She smiled, "Sure."

"How about a walk around Golden Gate Park? I've actually never been there."

"You haven't? Sure, we can do that."

Eli drove Angelina to the park in another unassuming rental car. He wore a hat and sunglasses and so far, had managed to evade being recognized…or at least, approached.

Eli couldn't remember the last time he'd taken a casual stroll in a park. He luxuriated in the experience; especially now that he had Angelina's calming presence beside him. It was an early spring day; a chill breeze caressed Eli's face as he reached to take hold of Angelina's hand.

"If I remember correctly, there are three more chakras you haven't told me about. I want to learn more. Please, can you tell me about them?"

Angelina grinned, "Yes, of course. I'd love to. After the heart chakra, there's the throat chakra, which represents our ability to communicate who we are—our feelings, our self-expression, our truth," she looked up at Eli thoughtfully. "Actually, Eli, your throat chakra is what drew me to you."

"Really? How so?"

"That first day in class, when you chanted 'om.' Something went through me. Your voice had the most beautiful resonance."

"Thank you."

"Now I understand…you're a singer. You have a powerful voice, Eli. You know, you can use that in many ways…"

Eli wasn't quite sure what she meant, but he didn't pursue questioning.

"Then there's the third eye chakra, which is our ability to focus and see higher meaning."

"I wish I had access to that one."

"You do, Eli. We all do. It's just a matter of paying attention…to our intuition." Angelina continued, "Then finally there's the crown chakra, which is the highest one, at the very top of our heads. It represents our ability to be fully connected spiritually. When we access this chakra, we experience pure bliss. Everything worldly falls away."

"Actually…I think I know what you mean. I've been in that state before when I'm playing music. It used to happen a lot more frequently when I was younger."

"I am not surprised. It's often easier for children to reach that state…they haven't been so programmed by the world yet. For adults, we have to work harder at it, through meditation or yoga, or art—like music. Or, some people try to take short cuts by taking drugs. I prefer natural highs, though, myself."

Eli thought of all the drugs he'd seen people take on the road. It was no wonder…the profession led so many people to feel, like Angelina had said, like zombies. He, himself had dabbled in drugs in order to attempt not just an escape from all his thoughts but to feel a deeper connection with the world. He had experienced high moments, for sure, but nothing compared to what he was able to cultivate through his music.

As if she read his mind, Angelina asked, "What's life like on the road? Do you get tired of all the traveling?"

"Life on the road is…chaotic. Sometimes it's the best feeling in the world, sometimes it's the worst. When I'm on stage, I try to completely lose myself in the music. Often, I'm unaware of the thousands of people before me. From the stage, the audience is dark; it's easy to imagine there's no one there.

"But sometimes it's also amazing to feel the energy of so many people in tune with what I'm playing. I have this… incredible power…to be able to communicate with so many people. A single note can make someone cry. One song can hold so much meaning to people…it can remind them of someone they lost in life, or a particular experience they had when listening to the song on the radio. It can offer someone respite from…human suffering. That's a responsibility that I don't take lightly.

"But then…other times, I want to leave it all behind. Not music. That will always be a major part of my life. But the culture around it…the go, go, go. The schmoozing. The interviews. As I said, nothing is private in my life. And because people believe that I'm supposed to be a role model for people, I have constant anxiety that I'm going to fuck up…that some kid is going to off himself because of some lyric I write. Or maybe I'll not be the nicest person…I'll break someone's heart because of my crazy lifestyle and damage them in some way, you know?" Eli looked anxiously at Angelina.

"I think I may know," she replied.

"Angelina, we talked about honesty. I want you to know exactly what you're getting yourself into if you decide you want to continue seeing me. I have a show at the Civic Center tomorrow night. Will you come?"

"I would like that."

"Great," Eli smiled. "I'd like you to watch from backstage.

I want you to see what I see...to feel what I feel from the stage...as much as you can, anyway."

"I will try."

"Thank you."

THE TWO SPENT A MAGICAL AFTERNOON TOGETHER WANDER-ing through the park, and sometimes just sitting and listening to the birds, the wind blowing through the leaves, and each other's breath. In some ways, Eli was reminded of his youth and the countless hours he had spent on the farm, highly observant of what was around him. He recognized how he'd lost a lot of his early sense of wonder.

Angelina, on the other hand, seemed able to notice subtle-ties even when engaged in conversation.

"How do you do that?" he asked.

"Do what?"

"You seem to look in the direction of a noise before the noise even occurs."

"Oh, that," Angeline laughed. "People tell me that all the time. But it's not that hard...it's a practice...like learning the guitar. Or writing music. If you're really present and paying attention, you'll notice when a bird is about to fly away, for example. Birds warn each other of our presence first."

Eli reflected on how sometimes he felt he could read the minds of his bandmates...or rather maybe he was simply pick-ing up on extremely subtle facial expressions or other body movements. It was true. It was a practice.

"What is your practice like?"

"Well, as you know, I do a lot of yoga, and also medita-tion. I practice meditation all the time...when I'm going for a walk or riding the bus. We can actually meditate anytime, anywhere. Just be still. As I mentioned, I like to ask myself, 'What is the quietest sound you can hear?' A few minutes of focusing on that question alters my state. Sometimes I miss my bus stop," Angelina laughed.

Eli felt he could lose himself in her laugh.

"Is that all? How else do you practice?"

"Well, I practice gratitude every day. I went through quite a dark period in my life before I decided to leave the ashram. Then a wise teacher told me that I was concentrating my thoughts mostly on things I wanted and didn't have, and I was completely forgetting what I already had. I had thought that what I had was something I was entitled to have. It sounds cliché, but I was taking a lot of things in my life for granted. So, my teacher encouraged me to keep a gratitude journal.

"Ever since then, I've kept a list that I add to every night before I go to bed and every morning when I first wake up. Writing makes your thinking visible. Sometimes I even draw pictures. Then when I'm done with my list, I say out loud, 'Thank you for another day to be alive and well.' It's important, however, that we don't just say 'thank you,' however. We need to *feel* grateful. And the feeling of gratitude must be genuine."

"Hmm," Eli nodded.

"Soon after I started practicing gratitude, I could see changes in my life. I started feeling more content and happy. I realized that, after all, my situation wasn't so bad; there were a lot of people in worse situations than mine. I reached the conclusion that it's not happiness that brings us gratitude, but it's gratitude that brings us happiness."

"That's really beautiful."

"It is," Angelina smiled.

"I would like to do the same as you. Most days, I feel like I have no time to sit still and just be with my thoughts. It's crazy when we're on tour. When we're recording, it's a bit easier…especially when I'm writing new material. But we'll be on tour now for several more months."

"The perfect time to start will never come. We have to make a conscious choice to start now, where we're at."

"Yeah, I suppose you're right."

"Do you remember me telling you about the heart chakra?"

Eli smiled. Did he ever.

"Let's practice now. Think of something you're grateful for," Angelina stopped and stood across from Eli, holding each of his hands in hers.

"Ok, got it."

"Now, in order to feel grateful, and not just think it, imagine your heart chakra," she raised one of his hands and placed it on his chest. "Close your eyes, smile, and picture a warm light coming from right here."

Eli took a deep breath. "It does feel warmer."

"Good. Now imagine that warmth spreading from your heart chakra all throughout your entire body."

"I'm trying, but I don't feel it outside of where our hands connect."

"Just wait. Give it time. Remember, it's a practice. Now stay still. Breathe. And keep picturing that warm light."

Eli wasn't sure if the heat generated from Angelina's touch on his body, or if he had conjured it himself, but he began to feel really hot.

"I feel it."

"Good! That's great. There's hope for you yet," Angelina joked. She lowered her hand from his chest and leaned forward to kiss Eli on the lips. He reciprocated, raising his hands to stroke her face gently.

"It's getting hotter," Eli smiled.

"True," she grinned back.

"Any chance you might want to…go back to your place?"

"I would like that," she smiled.

The two made their way to Angelina's apartment, and this time they didn't bother with warming up any tea. Their lovemaking was enchantingly different. Angelina told Eli with a smile that if he wanted to make love, they were going to do it her way this time. He was going to learn Tantra.

He was open to learning the new approach; the day had relaxed him and the slower pace was easier for him to adjust to this time around. Though he had to keep himself from reaching orgasm much longer than he usually would have liked, he had to admit the reward was a deeper sense of pleasure and intimacy. *Not having to hide who I am may have helped too*, he considered.

The two had dinner at Angelina's apartment—Angelina proved herself quite the vegetarian chef—and afterward stayed up late getting to know each other further. Upon waking up the next morning, however, Eli felt anxious. He had a gig in town that night, which meant he'd have to arrive at the venue late afternoon for sound check. Already, he could feel his mind slipping back into checklists and responsibilities; it felt like slipping into another identity.

Eli was nervous as well about Angelina being at his show. *What if she doesn't like what she sees?* But he wanted to be open with her. There was no sense building a relationship on a false foundation, he was aware.

After a nice brunch at Angelina's apartment that morning, Eli invited her to come with him to the Civic Center. It was not the largest venue he'd played, by any means, but the likes of Janis Joplin and The Grateful Dead had graced the stage in years past before audiences of nearly 6,000. Tonight, was a sold-out show, as usual.

Eli entered through the backstage door, escorting Angelina with him past security. Fans had already begun to line up at the main entrance, even though doors would not open for several hours yet. A few stragglers were hanging out by the tour bus, although a fence kept them at least fifty yards away. Nevertheless, they did not miss his arrival.

"Eli! Eli! Ahhh!!! Come here, we want to talk to you!"

"Ohmigod!! Eli, will you sign my ticket?"

Eli nonchalantly walked past. He did not want to encourage people to intrude on what was meant to be private space. He glanced at Angelina and noticed her apprehension.

"Are you all right?" he asked, as soon as they'd passed through the door.

"Yeah, yeah. I am. It's just…different."

"One day they'll be calling your name, Miss Famous Actress," he smiled.

"I can only wish," she smiled back.

Eli saw a few of his bandmates around the corner. "Come. I'd like you to meet my band." Eli placed his hand on the small of Angelina's back and led her to the green room.

"Eli! Welcome back, man," his drummer slapped him on the back. "I see why you've been busy," he smiled and gestured towards Angelina.

"Guys, this is Angelina. Angelina, the guys—Robert, Jimbo, Mark, and Nathan. And this is my manager, Russ."

Each member took turns shaking Angelina's hand and issuing a warm welcome.

"Very nice to meet you, Angelina," Russ nodded. "Now Eli, you're needed at the front of the house. The audio engineer wants to speak with you."

Eli gave a quick smile to Angelina, "Okay. I'll be back in a few. Please, make yourself comfortable," he gestured to the sofa and hurried off.

"Angelina, want to see a card trick?" Jimbo called her over.

"Hey back off man, she's Eli's girl. If she experiences your magic, you know she won't be able to resist," Nathan joked.

"Would you two stop? Eli's body is way better than either of yours. No girl that hot is going to go for guys like you," Mark chimed in.

"Shut up, Mark! You act like she can't hear you. Angelina, I apologize for my rude mate," Robert threw an empty paper cup at Mark.

"Whatever dude, you're just jealous because you can't get a girlfriend," Mark chided in return.

Their banter continued for several minutes. Angelina wasn't sure what to say or do. *Would Eli just get back here soon?* she thought. A minute later, he did.

"Hey," he kissed her cheek. "The guys haven't been giving you a hard time, have they?"

"Well, maybe a little," she smiled.

"Say the word, and they're out of the band," he whispered in her ear with a wink.

It wasn't the band Eli was worried about, however. It was after the show when the groupies would arrive. *Step by step*, he thought to himself.

"Sound check is in five, guys," Robin announced.

"Do you want to watch?" he turned to Angelina.

"Yes, of course," she smiled.

The band took the stage shortly; the only others in the huge auditorium were staff members of the venue, security, Eli's manager, and members of the stage and audio crews. Angelina could feel the anticipation in the air; everyone was bustling about, getting ready. She took a seat in the third row.

"Hello, hello, one two, one two," the sound engineer spoke into the mic. "That's good.

Eli, you good?"

Eli approached the microphone, "*Carried awaaay by the look in your eye...*" Eli sang before strumming his guitar lightly. "A little more reverb please, Tom," he gestured to the sound engineer.

Eli broke into a guitar riff, and Angelina recognized it immediately. *Haven't I heard that on a commercial?* she wondered.

"*Was it something I said...was it something you craved... Would it have hurt just as much...if I'd given it to you straight...*" Eli crooned. Angelina sat back in awe. No wonder he was famous. *That voice.* It melted her heart at the same time that it elevated her consciousness. He sang from so deep within... *what an old soul,* she thought.

For nearly twenty minutes, Angelina felt she'd been treated to a private concert - one that shook her to the core. She had heard some of his music on the radio before, but it wasn't at all like this. *There was something about live music,* she thought.

"Well, what do you think so far?" Eli asked her after he'd put down his guitar and made his way to where she'd been seated.

"I think...you're amazing," Angelina grinned.

"You're amazing," Eli smiled back.

"No, *you* are amazing," Jimbo approached from the side, laughing. "Alright, you two lovebirds. It's meal time. Come get some grub."

Catering had arrived backstage. Eli and Angelina made their way to the table where the rest of the band was getting seated. Angelina couldn't help but notice the abundance of meat. Although she was vegetarian herself, she held no judgment about those who ate meat, she simply observed that a diet like this on a regular basis must not lead to optimum health.

She sat through the meal regardless, nibbling on a salad. She was starting to feel anxious, and her appetite wasn't the greatest. *Maybe it's just all the testosterone in the air*, she considered.

After the meal, the opening band—who had been at the meal with them—did a short sound check, and more staff members from the venue began to arrive. Doors would open soon, and the place was abuzz. In addition to the main bar on the lower level, bar stands were being set up at every corner and around the balcony.

Angelina watched from a dark corner at the side of the stage as fans begin filtering in. The show was reserved seating, but even so, they had begun lining up hours before and came bursting into the auditorium to find their seats. The quiet ambiance Angelina had enjoyed during sound check gave way to booming popular music, preparing the crowd for a pulsating evening.

Everywhere, people held signs up that read everything from the likes of, "Eli, we love you!!" to song requests, to announcements regarding birthdays, and even—one that stood out to Angelina—messages of gratitude, "One year cancer free today. Your music got me through."

"Here they come," Eli spoke from behind the curtain. Angelina jumped a bit, shaken from the observation.

"Wow, Eli. These people really love you."

"Naww. They love my music. They love who they think I am. But they don't love me."

Angelina turned to him solemnly. Suddenly, she understood how hard it must be for someone like him to trust someone else's love. Looking back at the crowd, she noticed how young the audience was. And mostly female.

"Eli?"

"What do your parents think of all of this?"

"My parents? Well, they're proud of me. They've always supported me."

"I sense a 'but'…"

"Ha. Yeah, well…honestly, I don't see them very often."

"Why so?"

"Because I'm busy. Because sometimes I don't think they understand me…or my lifestyle. Because…sometimes I think I'm a disappointment to them…"

"But you just said they're proud of you."

"Yeah. That's true. Maybe it's me. Maybe I'm a disappointment to me. And talking to them makes me more aware of that." Eli hadn't consciously considered that possibility before. *Holy shit,* he thought.

"I'd like to meet them someday," Angelina said thoughtfully. Eli was silent. "Oh, God, sorry. I don't mean…I just mean I'd like to understand you better through them, that's all. I'm not trying to be that girl that moves too fast, that's not what I meant."

"I know," Eli replied. "But do you know what, Angelina?"

"What?"

"I should be so lucky if you were."

Angelina appeared shy for the first time since he'd met her. "In fact,…I'm falling in love with you."

It was Angelina's turn to remain silent, as Eli awkwardly fidgeted. "Sorry, I'm the one moving fast now. I shouldn't have told you that yet."

"No, it's not that. Don't apologize, Eli. I want you to be honest."

"Then what is it?"

"It's just…I think it's hard for someone like you…someone so 'rich and famous,' as you said…to have a strong spiritual practice. It's not impossible, but it's hard. And I'm afraid to be with someone who's not committed to a spiritual path."

"I'd like to be, Angelina. You're much further ahead than me, but I'd like to be where you are at."

Angelina looked back out at the audience; Eli remained a few feet away, still behind the curtain.

"I've been told that before. But wanting it is not enough. You have to *live* it. And how can you live a grounded, balanced life while being a rock star?"

"Didn't you say you want to be an actress? The lifestyle isn't necessarily much different."

"That can be true. Trust me, I've thought of that. But I want to act with purpose…"

"You don't think what I'm doing has purpose?"

"No, I didn't say that…" Angelina was struggling to find the right words. "I'm sorry. That's not what I meant. I just… need time."

"Come here," Eli motioned. Angelina hesitated. "Come,

please." Eli pulled her in for an embrace, placing her head tightly against his heart. "Do you feel that?"

"I feel your heart."

"Good. It's warm. And do you know why?"

"Why?"

"Because of your light. Because of your spirituality. It's what I love most about you. I would never discourage that or try to take it away."

Angelina felt a solitary tear stream down her cheek.

"I would love for you to give me a chance. Can you do that?"

"I think so."

Eli placed two fingers under her chin and tilted her face up to look in her eyes. "You think so?"

Angelina looked deep into his eyes. It was too late, she knew. She'd already fallen for him, too.

"I can."

"Thank you," Eli kissed the top of her head softly. "I have to join the guys. You can come with me or stay here if you like."

"I will stay here."

"Okay," Eli kissed her lips this time. "Take as much time as you need. When I come back, it will be to go on stage."

Angelina nodded and watched him as he walked off.

Angelina found a chair off to the side of the stage and remained there to watch the opening band. They were good, but they did not have the magical quality that Eli and his band had. There was a short set break after they left the stage, and Angelina remained seated, waiting for Eli to return to take the stage.

His band members came first; instantly, the audience erupted. What they had anxiously been waiting for was about to begin. The keyboardist kicked things off, and the room fell silent. Lead guitar filled the room, but from nowhere in sight. Suddenly, Eli stood in the dark beside her; she hadn't even seen him appear. He looked at her and winked as he stepped out from behind the curtain to grace the stage.

Everyone was on their feet; Angelina could see women in the front row crying. The crowd was jumping, together they seemed to generate a shared heartbeat. Angelina stood to get a feel for what Eli was seeing from center stage. Only the faces of the people in the front rows could be seen, the rest of the audience was a mass of energy and noise only.

She watched as Eli played to the room. His face would cringe in…ecstasy. It was a similar face she'd seen him make when they were making love. This is what he loved more than anything, there was no doubt. Voices flooded Angelina's head as she engaged in an inner dialogue with who she called God…

How can I compete with this?

You don't have to. He can love you AND love his music at the same time.

I know, but what about all these women? All these fans?

They are there to feed his purpose. You know this.

But why me? Why did he fall in love with me?

You represent what he's missing in his own life. Not just love, but a connection with something bigger. You have the opportunity to be a great teacher.

But what if I get hurt?

You cannot not live life simply because of the possibility of getting hurt. This is what you've wanted, too, Angelina.

I want to be an actress.

Yes, in order to be a greater teacher. Trust me, Angelina. I know what I'm doing.

Okay, I trust you.

Angelina finished watching the show. She watched as audience members tried to crawl on stage, and security pulled them down. She watched as women threw bras on stage—one that even landed on Eli's microphone. She watched as Eli evolved into someone she had not seen him be before—a chameleon, really, that at times took the form of an ego-driven commandant, other times a sensitive boy, and other times still a man so deeply absorbed in his music—his passion—that she swore she saw God through him.

"Yes," she whispered. "I trust you, God."

AND SHE DID. THAT NIGHT, AFTER THE SHOW, SHE MAIN-tained that trust as she watched Eli meet and greet what must have been a hundred members of his fan club—some who were so plastered they could barely stand up straight. She maintained her trust as one woman removed her shirt and asked Eli to sign her breast—and he did. She waited patiently until the line disappeared, and finally…finally, Eli put down his beer and his Sharpie and approached her.

"Thank you for waiting," he stated sincerely. "Sorry that took so long."

"It's fine. Is it like this every night?"

"Every night," Eli replied. "Can you handle that?"

"I think I can."

"Good," Eli chuckled, "Because sometimes I'm not sure I can."

Angelina could feel how tired he was.

"You know we have to pull out of here tonight, right?"

"Yes. Where to next?"

"Santa Barbara. Then L.A. Then overseas."

"Overseas?"

"Yep. London…all over Europe, really."

"When will you come back this way?"

"We don't tour through here for quite a while, but I will come back as soon as I can. You know, you can always join me where I'm at, too," Eli grinned before adding, "All expenses paid."

Angelina smiled, "I have my classes. And auditions…I don't know, Eli."

"Think about it."

"I will."

"Let me call you a cab home."

"Thank you."

"I'll tell you what…I'll call you, too. Every day, until I see you again."

"I'd like that," Angelina smiled.

Eli pulled her in close and kissed her passionately. "Thank you. For the most amazing weekend of my life."

Angelina thought of the night before, when they'd made love so deeply she had cried. She wasn't sure, but she thought he may have cried, too.

"I won't say what I want to say because I don't want to scare you," Eli smiled.

"I love you, too," Angelina winked. Eli felt he was in heaven.

"Eli! Get on the bus! We're moving," Russ called. "Angelina," he nodded, "Pleasure to meet you."

"I'll call a cab, don't worry about it," Angelina offered.

"You sure?"

"I'm sure."

Eli kissed her one more time. "Thank you for trusting me," he whispered, before turning and hopping onto the bus.

CHAPTER NINE

———∞∞∞———

THE MAN IN THE MIRROR

Eli had feared he would fail in his promise. He hadn't been unfaithful, but he'd sure as hell found it difficult to offer Angelina what he knew she deserved. For a while, he did call her every day. He'd also managed to fly to see her once a month, even if sometimes it was for less than twenty-four hours.

Angelina had agreed to visit him once in the past six months, as well. He'd flown her to meet him at a show in Mumbai—she'd confided to him early on in their relationship that she'd always wanted to visit India, and he went to extremes to allow for two open days in his schedule to spend time with her there.

When they were together, their relationship was easy. Her presence relaxed him; when he managed to set aside commitments to his career to be with her fully, he experienced a heightened sense of joy that rivaled what he felt on stage. Eli had seen so much of the world in his young life that before he met Angelina, he'd considered himself to have quite an advanced level of awareness of the world. She proved to him time and again, however, what an infant he was spiritually.

That realization was a hard pill for Eli to swallow. He'd been placed on a pedestal his entire life; fans continuously praised him not only for his musical prowess but his intellectual dexterity. The lyrics of his songs revealed a depth of emotional intelligence that Eli sometimes didn't feel he even deserved to give his name to a writer. Where did those words come from? He often wondered. Sometimes he didn't fully understand what they meant, but he knew they needed to be shared.

Despite his studies and experiences and his innate wisdom, he knew he had a lot deeper work to do to reach the level of spiritual advancement that Angelina sought in a partner and deserved as a companion and collaborator on her path. She was going places, he knew. And he didn't want to hold her back.

Slowly, he let more and more time pass between phone calls. It wasn't just he that found it difficult to find time to contact her or be with her; she was busy too. She'd recently experienced an influx of auditions and had secured a minor recurring role in a spiritual TV series. Sometimes when he called and left a message, it would be a few days before she would return his calls. He was proud of her though; she was following her dream.

Meanwhile, Eli's career reached even greater heights. There wasn't a magazine cover he hadn't been on, and often the image of him they conveyed—though not even accurate— was not one that was easy for Angelina to see. They had not publicly spoken of their relationship and had miraculously managed not to be photographed during the brief encounters that they had together, but that left the tabloids reaching for women to falsely pair him with.

One publication had even published a cover photo displaying his hand grabbing the rear end of a woman clad in a bikini. He could tell instantly it had been photo-shopped, but to the average uninformed eye, it offered convincing evidence that, if not dating, he was at least messing around.

Finally, Eli and Angelina mutually decided their relationship wasn't working—not now, not this way. Though it was a joint and compassionate decision, it was painful for each of them. Eli felt, in fact, that it was harder for him than it was for Angelina. He thought about her every moment his life slowed down enough for him to feel anything at all. Sometimes he didn't want to feel, and he'd self-medicate with a hit of marijuana. A small dose helped ease his recurring back pain as well, which had gotten worse in the past few months.

Tonight, he'd taken a few hits offered to him by a bandmate. He needed to ease some nerves; it was his 25th birthday, and he was playing Wembley Stadium in London. Ninety thousand people were in attendance in the sold-out arena; he could hear them all from backstage. Their cheers projected massive bolts of energy that shot through him at regular intervals. I can't believe I'm here, he thought. What a wild ride. Whatever emotional pain he'd felt earlier had subsided. I'm the fucking bomb; he thought to himself with a smile as he prepared to pump himself up to walk out on stage.

He observed the cue from his band that it was time. With a rush of adrenaline, he raised his arms above his head, his electric guitar strapped over his shoulder, as he walked to take his place in front of the microphone. He began his set with the title track of his new album, Shaken. The crowd went crazy, and he couldn't help but allow a wave of ego-driven pride to drift through his mind. The gravity of the night was not lost on him; he knew of several celebrities in attendance that would also be attending an opulent after-party in honor of his birthday—Carlos Santana, Ed Sheeran, Mick Jagger and Sir Richard Branson, to name a few.

His attitude humbled, however, as, towards the end of his set, Angelina crept back into his thoughts. He launched into the number one song he'd written for her, "I Fly to You." The song had been in the charts for the last four months, and it appeared everyone in attendance that night knew every single word. He watched their mouths move in perfect harmony; though he often liked to manipulate the way he sang certain songs live, this was a song he'd always performed in the same way.

The song was sacred to him, and it had also taken on a life of its own among his fans. His fan club manager had told him of the countless letters he'd been sent, sharing stories of love rekindled or born for the first time. It had already become one of the most popular contemporary love songs.

Tonight's performance, though, was different. Eli had been about to launch into the second verse of the song when a voice reverberated loudly in his head.

"Eli!"

It rang so deeply that he physically shook. He took a step back from the microphone, confused.

"Eli, I am here," it repeated itself twice. He was certain the voice was inside his head only, but where the hell did it come from? Eli began questioning his state of mind, Did I have one too many hits before the show? It was only marijuana, wasn't it? Did someone mess with it?

He was aware of his band repeating the intro to the second verse for the third time, waiting for him to enter. He suddenly couldn't recall the words, as he was so consumed by this strange voice in his head. Finally, Mark came over to the microphone and led the second verse off for him, "Last night when you told me you were crumbling from the weight…"

Mark made eye contact with Eli, as Eli nodded his head, shaken back to the present. The voice had finally subsided, and he managed to continue with the rest of the song and finish the last twenty minutes of the concert. He made it through an encore, as well, before retiring to backstage with a look of fury. He was disgusted with himself. God dammit, this was a big night, and I fucked it up, he thought.

His bandmates were more concerned than they were frustrated with him.

"Hey, what was the deal, man? Are you feeling alright?" Mark was the first to question him.

"Yeah, yeah, I guess so."

"What was going on in your head? You looked completely someplace else," Jumbo added.

Eli questioned if he should share what had happened, but finally decided he would.

"Honestly, there was something going on in my head. I heard this loud voice, saying my name. It completely caught me off guard…Hey, Jimbo, where did you get that marijuana, man? Did someone fuck it up?"

"Same source as always. It can't be that. I had the same stuff you did, and I'm fine."

"You're probably just stressed, Eli. It's a big night. But forget about all that now, it's over. The show was a hit, no matter what. Just relax. The fun is about to begin," Mark gestured to two young, blonde models who just walked backstage.

There would be no traditional meet and greet this night; instead, arrangements had been made for an exclusive VIP after-party to be held at The Lanesborough to celebrate his birthday. Invitations had been sent six months in advance, and these two Swedish Victoria's Secret models were among the list of guests his manager had arranged.

"Hi Eli," the two waltzed over to where he stood, draping their arms around his shoulders as each leaned forward to kiss one of his cheeks. "We have been looking forward to this evening. Happy birthday!"

"Thank you," Eli couldn't deny their beauty, but he was still feeling distracted and shaken from the incident with the voice in his head. He was also trying to suppress the feelings he still had for Angelina. He wished she was with him now; he was dying to hear her interpretation of what had happened out there on stage.

"Eli, the driver is here," his manager tapped him on the shoulder and gestured to a man in the doorway wearing a tailcoat. The man bowed as Eli made eye contact.

"Alright, I'm ready," Eli grabbed his jacket and nodded goodbye to the two ladies, who he knew he'd see later. The driver ushered him to the car—a sparkling new Rolls Royce Phantom that would bring him, his manager and his bodyguard to the hotel suite. The rest of the band would be taking the limousine parked behind his ride.

Every room at the hotel had been reserved for the occasion, despite the $30,000 a night per-room price tag. Eli was led to the seven-bedroom, Regency-style suite that would be his for the next two nights. He had been in many extravagant rooms before, but this one outdid them all. Twenty-four-carat gold leaf was everywhere his eyes landed; enormous chandeliers hung from the ceilings, and handcrafted furniture from Restall, Brown and Clennell were distributed comfortably around the room. Eighteen-century oil paintings hung from the walls; Eli felt like he'd stepped back in time to a palatial era in British history.

However, the room held modern amenities that could merely have been dreamed about at that time. Television screens were hidden behind the paintings, and everything was remote controlled, save the night lights that led the way to one of the suite's eight marble bathrooms once a foot hit the floor during darkness.

"I trust everything is to your liking, sir?" a hotel representative inquired.

"Yes, absolutely."

"Then I will leave you to your evening. You know where to inquire should you need anything. As you know, the party is being held in the banquet hall."

"Yes, thank you." The door was closed behind the man, leaving Eli a few precious minutes alone before he'd have to join the party downstairs.

This is an awfully big space for just one person, he thought. Again, he wished Angelina were with him now. Can I call her? He wondered, before deciding it was best not to. You have to get her out of your head; he criticized himself. Regardless, he pulled out his phone and scanned his missed calls. He noticed now that his parents had called him earlier in the day.

He listened to the voicemail, "Hi, Eli, it's Mom and Dad. We just called to wish you a happy birthday! We know you have your big event tonight, so we do not expect a callback, but just wanted to let you know we're thinking of you. We love you."

I could call them back now, he considered. It was 1 a.m. in London, but he figured only about 5 p.m. in Oregon. Just then, he heard a knock on his door. The band had arrived.

"Yo, Eli! Where you at? There's a room full of bigwigs waiting for you downstairs," Mike called through the door. Eli opened the door, "Hey, yeah, I'm coming." Eli slipped his phone back into his pocket and followed Mike to the elevator. I'll call them some other time, he thought.

As he entered the banquet hall, the room erupted into song, "Happy birthday, dear Eli, happy birthday to you..."

Eli allowed any lingering thoughts about his family or Angelina or the voice he'd heard earlier to dissipate as he joined the crowd. It was his birthday, and though he had a role to play as he schmoozed with the legendary rock stars and celebrities in attendance, he allowed himself to let loose. He didn't even try to brush off any of the adoring women that sought to rub shoulders with him, or sometimes more.

After a few hours of casual imbibing and general discourse, however, Eli felt socially and physically exhausted. He wanted to return to his room. He locked eyes with one of the blonde models from earlier in the night. As if on cue, she winked at Eli before tapping the other model on the shoulder and sauntering over to him with her friend.

"Hey, birthday boy," the two women said in unison. Wait, are they twins? Eli wondered with pleasurable anticipation.

"Hello, ladies. Do you care for a nightcap?"

"As you wish," the ladies linked arms with Eli as the three

of them exited discreetly and made their way to the elevator. As they reached the door to his suite, Eli entered the room code and held the door open, "After you," he gestured for the women to enter. "Make yourselves comfortable."

Eli made his way over to the bar, where he poured three glasses of Moet & Chandon Dom Perignon champagne. The fact that the bottle was in a plated white gold case and sold for nearly $3,000 hardly fazed him; he had become accustomed to such extravagance.

He returned to the sofa, where the two women sat and placed himself between them. "Cheers," they toasted to Eli's birthday and took a sip of champagne. Eli leaned back and closed his eyes. Had he not been so tired, there was no telling where the night might have led, but the women's attempted advances and their sheer beauty was no match for his exhaustion. He dozed in and out of consciousness; for a moment, he thought the hand going up his shirt was Angelina's, and he smiled. Before long, however, he fell into a deep, intoxicated sleep.

Eli wasn't sure how much time had passed when he woke up, having to use the bathroom. The ladies were each asleep beside him, and he noted gratefully that they were fully dressed. Two apologies I won't have to make, he thought.

He stumbled his way to the nearest bathroom and released the pressure in his bladder. Shaking away any excess drops, Eli refastened his pants and moved slowly over to the sink to wash his hands. He glanced at himself in the gold-leafed, oval antique mirror. You look like shit, man, he whispered to himself. He bent down to splash cold water on his face before looking back up at his image. No sooner had his eyes adjusted to the dim light, however, than they began playing tricks on him.

What the fuck? Eli blinked twice, but his image in the mirror continued to liquefy before him. Suddenly, the voice he'd heard earlier on stage returned, "Eli…Eli…Eli…" it rang loudly inside his head. Eli covered his ears; now certain someone had laced the marijuana he'd had earlier. Just when he thought things couldn't get any stranger, a face with a long neck began to protrude out from the mirror. Eli lost his balance and fell hard against the wall behind him, before sliding down into a seated position on the floor with his knees up to his chest.

Fuck I am hallucinating now…this is not good…

The face now spoke to him and continued to call out his name. Eli shouted back, "Go away! Stop! Leave me alone!" His frustration evolved to fear as he realized his body felt paralyzed.

Finally, the voice began to speak, "Please don't be scared, Eli. I am not going to hurt you. I am here to help you. My name is Michael, and I am your guide. We have a long journey ahead of us."

Am I dreaming? I don't understand. What is happening?! Eli had not spoken the words aloud, but his thoughts were read.

"This is not a dream, Eli. We made an agreement, which you do not now remember. I told you before that I would appear before you as your guide on the date of your twenty-fifth birthday."

Eli did not remember, but he felt a shift in energy that relaxed him. The voice no longer scared him. The room was alight now with a golden glow, and the face in the mirror appeared clearer and less intimidating. It was the face of a gentle man.

"Please, allow me to explain. I am here to awaken you to a higher consciousness, which is what you asked for in your previous life. You were a man of great wealth then, too, Eli. You—as a man named Derek Stryker—signed a contract that you would reacquire that wealth in your next incarnation. With wealth, comes great responsibility, however.

"Eli, you made choices in that lifetime that were not highly evolved. Every choice you make in each lifetime does not go unnoticed and must be balanced. Do you understand?"

"I...I'm not sure."

"It's okay. You will in time. We will be spending a lot of time together."

"What do you mean by 'a lot of time'?"

"I mean I will be with you as your guide for as long as it takes you to become awakened."

"What does that even mean?"

"It means, to understand that love is the greatest power."

Silence engulfed the room for a few moments before the man in the mirror continued, "I will come back. Look for me—but not in this form. You will know when you have found me."

The man registered Eli's look of puzzlement. "For now, get some rest. Go back to bed, Eli. Goodnight," and just as quickly as it had appeared, the face vanished.

Eli stood and reached his hand forward, placing his palm on the mirror. It felt normal. It looked normal, once again. What a messed up dream, he thought, though it had felt so real he wasn't sure if it was a dream, a drug-induced hallucination, or if that madness had actually happened.

Eli entered the living room and noticed the two women were still fast asleep. He walked slowly past them to his bedroom and shut the door. He wanted to be alone. Sprawling himself out on the king-sized bed, Eli turned the bedside lamp on and managed to fall back asleep.

CHAPTER TEN

THE VISITOR

Eli awoke before 7 a.m. the next day, feeling as though he hadn't slept at all. He was almost hesitant to step into the bathroom to shower, fearful that his experience with the mirror would reoccur. What did someone give me? He wondered. Whatever it was, the effects seemed to be gone now. No strange event or feeling occurred as he took a quick rinse and threw on some jeans, a t-shirt, and a jacket before lightly walking out of his suite, past the sleeping models once again, for a stroll.

Even the tourists seemed to be still sleeping at this hour. Eli followed a path through Buckingham Palace Gardens and was approached solely by a few wandering squirrels and pigeons, hopeful he might have a snack stashed away in one of his pockets. He continued on his way, passing boutiques and restaurants that hadn't yet opened for the day, until he reached the River Thames.

Eli leaned against the railing and gazed into the water. He felt a cool breeze on his face, making him wish he'd brought a scarf. Aside from fatigue, his mind remained rather unsettled. Perhaps it was the incident in the night, he thought, or maybe it was some existential crisis—does a quarter-life crisis even exist? He was so deeply engulfed in his thoughts that he didn't notice the man now standing beside him.

"Don't you just love the hour after dawn?" the man spoke in a posh, British accent.

The voice startled Eli. He looked to his left to notice an older gentleman, perhaps around sixty, who stood leaning on the railing beside him. He wore a long, gray trench coat and, like Eli's suite at The Lanesborough, harked of an earlier era. Eli preferred to be alone with his thoughts, but the man wouldn't let up.

"It's filled with so much promise ahead. Anything can happen that day…something that may even alter your life completely, you know?"

"Hmm," Eli shrugged, conveying disinterest.

"Unfortunately, humans are often too busy running through their to-do lists for the day, that they miss the real reason they are alive." The man paused before continuing, "Do you know the real reason you are alive?"

Eli made eye contact with the man. What is this guy's deal? He thought. Can't he tell I don't want to talk? "Let me guess; you're going to tell me."

The man laughed, "How wise you are. Indeed. You are here on earth—everyone is here on earth—to become awakened," he paused again before adding, "and to understand that love is the greatest power."

Eli's heart started to race. What the fuck? Those are the words from my dream…or hallucination, or whatever the hell that was last night.

The man reached out his hand, "Michael."

Michael. Eli glanced down at the hand before him. It

looked real. He was afraid that if he touched it, his hand might go right through it, which would most certainly freak him out. The man couldn't be real...that would mean that what happened last night was real...and what the hell would that mean?

But he had to know. Eli tentatively reached out his hand and clasped onto the one outreached before him. It was real.

"No need to introduce yourself. I know all about you, Eli."

Dammit. What the hell? He knows my name. Wait, does he just recognize me from the media? Surely that's it. This guy is just a quack.

"I'm not a quack, Eli. I am your guide. Remember? We met last night."

Shit shit shit. He can read my thoughts.

"No reason to be frightened, Eli. No one's thoughts are truly private. There's nothing I haven't heard before. But don't worry, it's not possible to offend me."

"What is this all about? Who are you?"

"Again, I am your guide to lead you to a higher consciousness. Everyone has guides, Eli. But I am here before you because you have been given a great responsibility in this lifetime—and we made an agreement that I would help you to not stray from your path."

"Why me? Why are you saying I have been given a great responsibility?"

"You are a man of great wealth and fame. You have the power to influence millions of people. There is grave responsibility in that position and an abundance of opportunity. You are quite blessed, Eli."

Eli considered how that realization had not gone over his head completely.

"It has taken you many lifetimes to reach the status you have now. You are an old soul, my friend."

"Many lifetimes? You keep saying that. Who are you saying I was before?"

"Yes, approximately 300 human lifetimes, not counting the lifetimes you've spent evolving from organisms to animals to an actual, functioning human being. There is nothing and no one you haven't been. In some of your human lives, you were stillborn, in some you died as a young child, and in others, you lived to be over one hundred. You have been the priest, the villain, the prostitute, the king, and…the rock star.

"But I am not here to talk about the specifics of these past lives; if you saw what you went through in those lives, there are images that would haunt you rather than serve you. It is best if you are only aware of who you are here, now."

"Okay, so I'm super-evolved…then why do I need you?"

"Careful, Eli. Do not let ego interfere with your lessons. It is important to understand that no matter how many lifetimes one lives, every being is on an equal plane. Earth is a school room of all grades present; a first grader would not be considered an inferior human being simply because he does not understand calculus."

Michael paused to allow time for Eli to process that idea before continuing. "In any case, you don't 'need' me, Eli. You could continue repeating the same mistakes lifetime after lifetime, and it would make no difference to me. You must understand, however, that what you resist, persists. Your species will suffer greatly if you and others continue to live in such a cycle. In fact, such a decision would be a disgrace to the great opportunity you have been given to reside here on earth."

Petra Nicoll

"If it is such a great opportunity, then why are so many people suffering? I personally live a privileged life, I know, but look around," Eli gestured to homeless people camped out on nearby benches. "There is poverty and pain everywhere. Would that man over there say it's a great opportunity to be here on Earth? Or what about people over in Syria right now? Or North Korea?"

Just then, Eli's body shivered as sharpened visions entered his mind. In a matter of nanoseconds, he watched image on top of image shoot through his mind of hurricane struck Porto Rico gradually rebuilding itself until becoming a beautiful and pristine land with clean and safe cities and smiling people.

"That is what is possible, Eli, if people like you step up."

"And if not? What if I want nothing to do with you?"

"Must I remind you that you asked for this."

"Bullshit. I have no memory whatsoever of asking for some crazy person to enter my head and morph out of my fucking bathroom mirror."

"Suit yourself, Eli. But I must warn you that if you ignore me and what I have come here to teach you, life will only get much, much harder—for everyone, including you."

At that moment, new visions entered Eli's mind of what appeared to be hell on earth. Lands were arid, completely void of soil capable of growing food. People were starving to death, coughing out the polluted air they were breathing in. All of the earth's animals had already died and been eaten by those who had maintained the highest rank in society. Now, however, everyone was on an equal, miserable plane, where each awaited his own death with yearning.

"Alright, alright, I get it. Please stop."

"Now do you understand the urgency of this matter? Those images you saw were not from very far in the future. Every moment, in fact, that we stand here talking instead of taking action brings life on earth closer to the reality you just witnessed."

Eli ran his fingers through his hair and shook his head, trying to cleanse himself of the terrible discomfort his body had just experienced.

"Are you ready to learn what I have come here to teach you? It will require daily study."

"I don't know, man. When the hell do I have time to meet with you? If you're so all-knowing, then you know what my life is like."

"Meeting with me will not interfere with your career. There are, however, other activities you engage in daily that are not bringing you closer to an awakening. I trust you know the activities I am referring to."

Eli could imagine a few. "Fine, so how does this work? Do we need to meet somewhere or something?"

"I will come to you."

"When? When will you come to me? I don't want you to scare the shit out of me like you did last night."

"From now on, I will come in human form, just as I am now. At times, you will see me when others will not. If we need to be discreet, we can communicate with thoughts and visions, rather than with words," Michael continued, "Are you ready to begin today?"

"Today? I have a rehearsal with my band this morning— I'm probably already going to be late—a photo shoot this afternoon, and then I'm meeting my manager and some executive for a new business venture, and I'm supposed to have drinks tonight with a gorgeous woman I met last night... Cherise? Cheryl? I don't know. The name is on my phone."

"Perhaps Cherise-Cheryl isn't as important right now as the state of the planet."

"Aww come on, man. Okay, fine, fine. I'll meet with you then. Say 10:00 p.m."

"And so, it is. I look forward to seeing you then, Eli," Michael tipped his hat, and Eli watched him fade into the London fog.

***

Eli was exhausted by the time 10 p.m. rolled around. The night before and the subsequent morning had left him energetically and emotionally depleted. He'd pushed through the mental cloudiness he'd felt all day to carry on with the responsibilities of his career.

He'd feigned focus during the band's rehearsal that morning; he'd smiled or otherwise gazed alluringly into the camera for every pose the photographer had positioned him in; over dinner, he'd closed a $500,000 business deal with a clothing line.

Now—just when he wanted to distract himself from being "Eli, the rock star" by imbibing and romping with a beautiful woman, he had to meet instead some ghost or something to talk about "higher consciousness"?

He probably won't even show up, Eli thought to himself as he paced back and forth in his London suite. His thought was interrupted, however, by the sudden appearance of Michael before him.

"Ah!" Eli jumped. Why do you keep doing that?!"

"I didn't mean to scare you. It's 10:00 p.m., is it not?"

"Yes, but couldn't you knock or something?"

"I'm sorry, I'm so used to appearing as we do in celestial form, rather than human. Next time I can knock if you'd like."

Eli gave Michael a sideways glance. "What are you doing here, anyway? I mean, what are you here to teach me or whatever?"

"Tonight, I will teach you two lessons that are interconnected. The first lesson is the concept of free will."

"Free will?"

"Yes, every human has it. It's the ability to choose freely between different thoughts and actions. It's an important concept to understand, and one you humans tend to misunderstand completely. If humans understood that everything that happens in their lives is the result of their own free will, there would be no one and nothing outside of themselves to blame for anything that doesn't 'go their way.' Free will means claiming responsibility for our lives and our shared planet. Are you following me, Eli?"

"Not really. I mean, this goes back to our earlier conversation today—I know I've been dealt an easy hand, so it's easy for me to claim responsibility for my good fortune. But what about people born into poverty and pain? Are you saying they are responsible for the economic or physical factors they were born into?"

"How do you know they didn't ask to be born into such a situation, just like you asked in your previous life to be born into the situation you are living now? How do you know that those experiencing the illusion of poverty or pain are not doing so to fulfill their purpose in that lifetime? In fact, the purpose that will lead them to a higher consciousness?"

"Why do you say 'illusion'? You can't deny that the degree of suffering on this earth is real."

"You are speaking of an illusion—the illusion of hell on earth. Every sentient being comes to understand at the moment of death that in life they had been given the gift of free will—and that some, in fact, had used it to create a hell on earth in their minds and their experiences.

"This is lesson number two, in fact: Hell does not exist—on earth, or in the afterlife. I know many of your human spiritual writings like to use this place of eternal torment and damnation as a manner to control your people, but I am here to teach you that there is no such place.

"What you call God is really the essence of pure, unconditional love—and unconditional love leaves no room for judgment or punishment. So then how, might I ask, could this 'God' create a place of such suffering?

"It is true that suffering feels real—in the experience of those who 'suffer,' it is. What happens is some people feel they deserve to suffer. Thus, they do. Maybe it is their religious doctrine that has told them so, or maybe it's a parent or teacher. Every human on earth was born with the opportunity to decide what to do and experience individually. That individual free will is then joined with collective free will—or the combined decisions of all individuals—which creates the experience you have here on this planet."

"What about after death? How can you be sure suffering does not exist in the afterlife for those who committed horrible acts here on earth?"

"I know because I've been there, Eli. Even members of the living among you had testified of what they experienced in a near-death moment, or a moment when they were clinically pronounced dead before coming back to life. Some of these people speak of having entered a place of pure love and beauty;

others speak of a place you might describe as hell. The truth is, whatever one expects to experience in life, is what one will experience at the moment of death.

"However, it does not take long before he or she who has 'died' recognizes that his or her experience can instantly be changed with a change in thought. If, upon experiencing what feels like hell, the being considers, 'I am leaving this place,' it will instead experience the truth of its being—which is the energy of pure love and light."

"You make it sound so simple."

"I promise you, it is. You humans overcomplicate things with confusing thoughts— mixed messages and ideas about how things are or are not, or should or shouldn't be. You have forgotten who you are, where you came from, and what you asked for in this life. But that forgetting is not unintentional, mind you."

"So, let me see if I have this straight—you, or God or whatever, makes us forget to remember? That makes no sense."

Eli, did you ever hear the phrase, "Unless you become as little children, you will not enter the kingdom of heaven?" "What do you think that means? "

"Wasn't it Jesus that said that?"

"Yes, it is written in the scriptures, not only the Bible!"

All the Master's and enlightened ones have given us this message since the beginning of time, but people often don't understand what it really means.

"Are you telling me I have to become innocent like a child or something?"

"There is a big difference between innocence and purity. Wisdom is purity because you have to become compassion-ate to have true wisdom. As long as there is stored disruptive emotion in the body, it is impossible to be truly wise. Clearing stored emotion is essential for living a happy, joyful life. Transmuting low frequency emotion of fear and sadness into love and joy is part of the magic of a particular meditation we will soon be studying."

I had pretty awesome parents who never argued and who loved me unconditionally, so I don't think this applies to me."

"Yes, Eli that is correct but you still absorbed some energies from what your parents experienced from their parents and their parents before them. "

"Ohmigod, that means nobody ever gets out of this emotional roller coaster, right?"

"Not exactly!" There are ways to move beyond these emotional blockages. One of your teachers, "Eckhart Tolle," calls it: "Pain Body" and it is truly painful to be stuck in negative emotion. Once a person has incarnated on earth several times, the question will eventually arise? "Why am I here, and who am I?

Everyone on earth experiences some form of anger, frustration, sadness, fear, loneliness and shame that began from the time of conception until the age of six. In these formative years the mind is in a theta brainwave state; the same brainwave as hypnosis. All the emotional energy felt during that time is assimilated directly into the subconscious mind and body. These emotions become the foundation of a world view that have run on autopilot all of your life, until now. Imagine a child at age 2, his or her parents may have felt anger, perhaps even arguing over financing or something in the child's presence. The powerful force of this anger was felt. Open and vulnerable to this powerful force from the parents, this vibration was stored in the aura or energy body of the child. The vibration is carried through life, continuing to create angry situations and relationships until this energy has been cleared. The child feels anger at age 8, again at age 10, age 16, then at 23, and so on. One may perceive the anger as a result of a relationship breakup, losing a job, an argument with a friend. This is the story, however. In fact, the stored vibration of anger has been there all along creating the story. Clearing the anger now, will cleanse the aura and body, transmuting anger into power and more joy forevermore. There is a type of meditation which empowers people to dive into the subconscious using a special frequency to heal old programs."

"Let me guess, you are going to teach me this, right?"

"If you humans remembered everything you've ever known and everywhere you've ever been, you'd be on information overload. Access to all of the knowledge of the universe would distract you from your purpose here on earth—which is to reach that stage of enlightenment yourself so that you can return and help others discover what you have learned. There are many souls lost here on earth, which is what is contributing to what you call suffering on your planet."

"Then why don't we all just return to earth as all-knowing angels, or guides? Why bother becoming human again and going through that whole process of forgetting and remembering and suffering?"

"Some people do decide to come back as guides—like me. But the earth needs human guides as well, to be able to relate to those in need at their level in a form they understand. You may recall having met some advanced teachers in your lifetime. Does anyone come to mind?"

No more than a moment passed before Angelina popped

into Eli's mind. Ohmygod. "Angelina," he said under his breath.

"Very good. It was no coincidence that you two crossed paths, Eli. She had many lessons to teach you, but you weren't ready for most of them. Now, can you think of anyone else in your life who has had great lessons to teach you? Lessons perhaps from another realm?"

Eli reflected on his youth. "I don't know. My music teacher?"

"Ahh. Your music teacher did teach you many important concepts of art and even geometry and science—pieces of the bigger puzzle, if you will. But there are two very enlightened teachers you've had in your life. Your whole life, in fact."

"Wait...Mom and Dad?"

"Why the hesitation, Eli?"

"Well, I mean, they always seemed so...simple. Just, you know, normal people."

"By which standards do you base what or who is 'normal,' Eli? And who says that 'simple' people can't be great teachers? In fact, people who have reached advanced levels of awareness often choose to simplify their lives, because they recognize the insignificance of material goods or the excess of choice your culture insists on selling. Your parents understood that the true meaning of life was in the present—in moments spent with loved ones, being still in nature, treading lightly on the land. They also recognized the importance of music—and its ability to heal."

"Ability to heal?"

"Yes, of course. Where do you think you'd be without music, Eli?"

"Well, I do know what it's offered me. It's my life."

"It's not all about you, Eli. In fact, none of it is. Do you think it's by coincidence that you were given this great talent?"

"I worked hard for the talent that I have."

"Yes, you did. I commend you for that. But you were chosen to have that ability, Eli. It is through your music that it was agreed you would be of great service to this planet. But that is a discussion we will have later. We have more lessons to get through first. But that is enough information for now. We will meet again tomorrow."

"Tomorrow? How many times are we going to meet?"

"Until you have learned what you need to learn."

"Yeah, yeah, okay. Well, tomorrow is busy."

"Again, Eli? I trust you can make time."

"You do realize I'm changing my life around for you, don't you? Normally this evening I'd be having great sex with somebody. Instead, I'm sitting here talking to some old man."

Michael laughed, "There are beings much, much older than me, Eli, and I would consider it an honor to be as wise as they. Now, what is your day like tomorrow?"

"I'm meeting my trainer for a workout at 9 a.m., then lunch with my manager to discuss PR for the rest of our Euro tour, then I'm flying with the band to Brussels for our gig tomorrow night."

"Well, then it seems we'll have to meet early in the morning. I'll see you at 7 a.m."

"7 a.m.?! You're crazy. No one in this business gets up that early."

"You did yesterday."

"Well, yeah, but that's because I couldn't sleep. Mostly because of you, I might add."

"I will ensure you sleep well tonight. We have a big job

ahead of us, Eli, and it needs your attention now. Now, go to bed. Tomorrow we will discuss the devil."

"I can hardly wait," Eli said sarcastically.

"Good night, Eli." Michael must have forgotten his promise to enter and exit as a human would; he appeared to dissolve straight through the closed door.

ELI DIDN'T NEED TO SET THE ALARM. MICHAEL KNOCKED ON his door at precisely 7 a.m. the next morning.

"Eli, good morning!" he called.

Eli begrudgingly threw the covers off to the side of his bed and made his way to the door, suppressing a yawn.

"Michael. I should have known you'd be prompt."

"How did you sleep?"

"Actually, not bad. But it's early. Don't you sleep? Where do you go when you're not annoying me?"

"Well, I don't have to sleep. I don't have to travel, either. I just close my eyes and consciously think of where I need to go, and I am there. So, in theory, I am everywhere."

"You have to share with me how that works."

"First things first. I promised we'd talk about the devil today. Shall we begin?"

Eli had already begun making coffee. "Sure, go ahead."

"Okay, so lesson three. The devil exists—but not as your scripture describes."

"Wait, last night you said that hell doesn't exist."

"True, true. Except in your mind. Similarly, the devil resides in a different form than you'd expect... 'he' is merely energy. Negative, of course. As you may recall, each atom that makes up all of life consists of both positive and negative energy. The negative part can be called the 'devil,' and the positive part can be called 'God.' Now, thoughts can also be negative or positive. Guess who controls each?"

"Sure, God controls the positive and the devil controls the negative."

"Correct. Now, what did we talk about yesterday—what is God?"

"The essence of pure love."

"Precisely. So, what is the devil?"

"Hate?"

"Almost. What controls hate? Go deeper."

"Fear."

"Bravo! The 'devil' therefore uses fear—fear of poverty, fear of old age, fear of loss of love, and so forth, to control one's mind with negative thoughts. School teachers, religious leaders, and parents often use fear as a tool to implant children with the fear of 'hell'—the greatest of all fears. Unbeknownst to them, they are feeding the devil's agenda to control the minds of future adults, leading to the chaos and discontent you are witnessing on your planet.

"Now, aside from those individuals who influence our early lives, as adults, the biggest trap people fall into that prevents them from experiencing themselves as pure love is their tendency to wander—or in another word, procrastinate. These people allow circumstances outside of their mind to do their thinking for them. They do not exercise lesson number one—the existence of their own free will—and use that free will to facilitate positive thoughts and therefore experiences. Are you with me?"

"Yes, I think so."

"Good. Now, people demonstrate their lack of free will when they allow their thoughts and inaction to be ruled by the influence of the media, of fellow procrastinating peers, and their fear. They are not engaging in behavior that is for their best interest; for example, they are not eating healthy foods in correct quantities, they continue working in a job they do not enjoy, they spend impulsively, and they do not love freely.

"As a result, these people 'suffer' from lack of purpose in life, lack of pleasure, lack of control. They make the same mistakes over and over again or are indecisive. They focus on the shortcomings of others instead of the ways they can improve.

"On the flipside, people who lead purposeful and pleasurable lives focus on thoughts and behaviors that are for their best interest—they know what they want, and they follow well-organized plans to achieve their goals. These are leaders, not followers; they are generous to others and expect nothing in return. They blame no one but themselves for things that do not go their way, and they take action to correct what went wrong to not repeat the same mistake.

"These are the people around whom others feel good; you may sense an aura or a warm light when you are around them. They inspire you, lift you up."

Eli's thoughts once again drifted to Angelina.

"So, you see, Eli, how all of these lessons are interconnected?"

"I do. But give me some direction, here. What are small, attainable ways to stray from the temptation of negative thought?

"I am glad you are thinking in this way. The first is to be very careful of who you surround yourself with, whether it is your friends, colleagues, or your choice for a partner. This includes your bandmates, and even your fans, Eli. It is important also to stay busy."

"Well, that one's taken care of."

"Wait—it's important to stay busy by occupying your mind and your time with the expression of positive, creative thoughts. Otherwise, that space will be filled with negative thoughts. Therefore, allow your music, your creative energy, to be a vehicle for positive thoughts and feelings.

"Use those positive thoughts to convert any adversity into a benefit. Always, always think for yourself. Question what is presented to you as opinion or fact, even when it comes from a person in a position of authority—in fact, especially then.

"Focus on the bigger picture of what you want from life—what is your greater purpose, beyond being a rock star—and sacrifice for it. Quiet your mind sometimes, and listen only to your heart."

I can do that, Eli thought.

"Good. That will be all for today." Eli did not see Michael evaporate, for his eyes were closed.

CHAPTER ELEVEN

A PURPOSEFUL LIFE

Eli had only gone to bed three hours before. His bladder was full of the beers he'd imbibed after the previous night's gig, and he begrudgingly stumbled out of bed to make his way to the bathroom. For a few moments, he forgot where he was. London? Manhattan? Where was the bathroom, anyway?

He caught a glimpse of a tall green bottle from the night before, Brasserie Cantillon. Ahh. Brussels, he remembered. He vaguely recalled having hooked up with a girl backstage the night before. A Belgian beauty, he grinned.

Eli's pants were already halfway down by the time he reached the toilet. A quick glance in the mirror made him jump and pull his pants back up, however.

"What the hell are you doing here?!" Eli exclaimed, more frustrated than he was scared.

Michael set the magazine he'd been reading aside and stood up from the comfortable position he'd assumed on the chaise lounge chair in the bathroom.

"Oh! You're up early. I was just waiting for you to be ready for today's lesson."

"Today's lesson? At this hour? It's still dark! And whatever happened to your plan to knock? You can't just hang out in my hotel bathroom at all hours of the night like this…What the hell, Michael?!"

"That's a great starting point to recap our previous lesson. What is hell, Eli?"

"Very funny."

"It wasn't a joke. Are you ready to begin?"

"Can't you see I have to pee? And I'm not done sleeping. It was a…late night last night."

"Yes, I do recall. Old habits die hard, don't they my friend?" Michael grinned but stepped out of the bathroom to allow Eli some privacy. "I'll be here, waiting for you to be ready. Rest as you must."

Eli took care of nature's call and attempted to ignore Michael's presence as he made his way back to bed. After twenty minutes of tossing and turning, however, he finally threw the covers aside and joined Michael in the sitting room.

"I can't sleep with you here, so we might as well begin."

"Excellent! Now, do you remember where we left off yesterday morning?"

"I don't know. It's early, Michael. Remind me."

"We were discussing how to redirect negative thoughts into positive thoughts by focusing on one's greater purpose."

"Ah, yes. Listening to our hearts."

"Indeed. Well done. Today's lesson will revolve around this topic—it is my favorite one, in fact."

"What is it?

"Knowing oneself."

"I already know myself."

"Ah, yes, I thought you would say that. That is why it is my favorite subject."

"Ok, what are you getting at?"

"Knowing yourself isn't as easy as you think it is. I am speaking of knowing yourself on a soul level—beyond the external, physical body or the personality. The only way to know yourself on this level is if you had insight into who you were in every single lifetime. You would need access to what is programmed into your memory on a cellular level from those lifetimes.

"To know yourself, you must understand all of your strengths and weaknesses. You must know that which you desire most in life. You must be aware of what makes you unique, what your likes and dislikes are, and what your limits are. To know yourself, you must know your life's purpose." Michael paused and leaned forward.

"How many people on the planet do you think are living a purposeful life?"

"Probably 50%."

"Ah, Eli…it is unfortunately less than 1%."

"Wow," Eli sighed. "I admit, that's a sad statistic. But I have found my passion, so I'm not sure why this applies to me."

"You may have found your passion, Eli, but have you found your purpose?"

"Isn't it the same thing? It's to make music."

"What kind of music, Eli?"

"I don't know. Music that moves people."

"True. But moves them to do what?"

"I don't know…to feel happy."

"It goes much deeper than that, Eli. But we will get to that later. You are not yet ready."

"Whatever," Eli resented the judgment.

"Watch your ego, Eli. It is not a judgment. It is an observation."

Michael leaned back into the couch, "Now, let's continue. Even though very few people are living a purposeful life, people on your planet are always asking, 'What is my purpose in life?' That is a good sign—to have the desire to understand one's purpose is the first step to uncovering it.

"In fact, all life forms have a purpose—whether it's a plant that produces food or an insect that pollinates the plant. The challenge is that humans become so enraptured in their mind chatter and their daily activities that they miss the purpose that is right in front of them.

"Some people also confuse 'success' with 'monetary wealth' as a sign that they are living their life's purpose. It is only when they reach their definition of success and still feel empty that they begin to wonder if they, in fact, have been living their life's purpose. Does that feel familiar to you, Eli?"

"It does."

"I thought so. The consequence of not finding one's purpose goes beyond dissatisfaction—it can even lead to disease if left unattended for too long."

"But I still don't see the difference between passion and purpose. If I have found my passion and it makes me and others happy, isn't that my purpose?"

"Perhaps. But do not confuse happiness with purpose. Happiness, as experienced in daily life, is situational. It fluctuates. Purpose is deeper. It is constant. It is an underlying sense of peace that cannot be altered, no matter your external circumstances."

"Tell me, Eli. Are you happy? Always, and no matter what?"

"I guess not."

"That is why we have work here to do together."

"Ok, I want to do the work. But how do I begin?"

"Again, you must first know yourself. Know your true values, your suppressed desires. You must also let go of the ego, or in other words, 'get out of your own way.' By doing so, you will learn your capacity for love, empathy, and generosity. And, you must use your creative energies to serve something larger than yourself.

"When you give simply for the sake of giving—without expecting anything in return—you will be in alignment with your purpose. The more you consciously engage in thoughts, emotions, and behaviors with positivity—with kindness, compassion, empathy, and a spirit of giving—the more you are keeping your ego at bay and, therefore, are able to know yourself and your purpose with greater clarity."

"Okay, so staying positive is easy, again, for people who 'have it all.' But what about the people who are suffering?"

"Do you believe you 'have it all,' Eli?"

"Well, I guess I do through some people's eyes."

"Do you suffer?"

"Not like other people do. I mean, not like people living in poverty or war. But...as we said, I'm not always happy either."

"Remember, suffering is merely a point of view. It can be used as a tool, Eli, to awaken one to his or her life's purpose."

"I don't get that."

"All around you are examples of people who have turned tragedy into tools for change. Someone may hear a story on the news about victims of human trafficking, for example, and be so moved by the story that they discover their life's purpose in helping victims of these situations. Even the loss of one's own child as a result of a hate crime can be used to spark one's purpose of educating others about tolerance."

Michael could sense Eli's hesitation in accepting that perspective. People so often struggle with this one, he shook his head.

"Allow me," Michael placed his hands on either side of Eli's head. Instantly, rapid-fire images were transferred into Eli's consciousness that portrayed an array of traumatic events—people losing everything in fires and floods, victims of abuse, and fatal car accidents.

Eli was suddenly overcome by grief. He was allowed, however, to experience the passage of years within an instant, and from there the grief subsided and was replaced by a sense of acceptance, calm, and purpose. He saw and felt the strength of the survivors as they spoke to large crowds and even individuals, educating them, inspiring them, and creating a ripple effect of others being awakened to their life's purpose.

Michael slowly removed his hands, "Now do you understand?"

Eli shook, allowing what he'd just experienced to sink in. "Ok. I suppose that makes sense."

"Good. Then let me introduce lesson number five, which is the importance of giving and receiving. I already mentioned the importance of service to something greater than yourself. There are many different ways to give—there are emotional gifts, such as your deep care for another, and the truth of who you are. Then there are physical gifts, such as the gift of your time, your work, and your money.

"Each of these is an important way to be of service, but equally important is to remember the importance, also, of receiving. You have demonstrated your willingness to give—I have seen you perform at multiple charity events and offer generous donations. But let me ask you, Eli—do you allow yourself to receive?"

"I'm not sure if I get what you mean."

"Receiving from another person is part of the dynamic of a relationship. How do you feel when you give to someone else?"

"I feel...good. It gives me great joy to make someone else happy."

"Good. And how do you feel when you receive?"

"Guilty, I guess. I have so much in my life that it's hard for me to accept gifts from others."

"I have noticed that. And not only physical gifts, Eli, but emotional gifts. You have a hard time letting love in, you know."

"Do I? I guess I never thought about it."

"Your parents are always offering you love, Eli. They do it when they call you, even if you don't answer. They do it when they come to your shows, because not only do they want to support you, but they want to offer you the gift of their time. But you do not accept their time. And there is another kind of love; not the kind the women on the road give to you for one night only...I am talking about the kind of love that seeks nothing in return. No boost to the ego, or to pride, or to one's wallet. The kind you were offered by a woman once..."

"Angelina."

"Yes. You gave your love to her, it's true. But you did not allow yourself to receive her love, as deeply as you could. But here is another question...why do you feel guilty receiving the gift of love, when you know firsthand that there is no greater feeling than to be able to offer someone else the feeling of being loved? By not receiving love, you deny someone else that pleasure."

"I never thought of it that way."

"I suggest you begin now. When you allow that realization in, Eli, you will discover that each human being is both separate and distinct from one another, and one with each other—through the process of both giving and receiving."

"That's deep," Eli ran his fingers through his hair as Michael laughed.

"And that's only the beginning. I will leave you with a lighter topic before you continue with your day, and that is lesson number six. The importance of gratitude. Gratitude is the key to increasing long-term life satisfaction. You may understand gratitude as the verbal expression of thanks and appreciation. However, gratitude is an emotion."

"Explain that."

"Of course. When one feels gratitude, he or she experiences a pleasant emotion. If one feels ingratitude, he or she experiences nothing. Therefore, by developing a practice of maintaining a grateful perspective, one increases his or her life satisfaction, or happiness, if you will.

"By the way, I say 'practice,' because gratitude can, in fact, be considered a skill. One must practice the intensity or depth of emotion that is felt through gratitude, as well as the frequency or ease in which grateful feelings are brought forth. Also, the span—or the number of different things and the number of different people for which one can be grateful for—contribute to one's level of life satisfaction.

"A person's level of spirituality and conscientiousness positively correlates with his or her ability to live a grateful life, and thus a purposeful life. Alternatively, one's attachment to materialism negatively correlates to his or her ability to be grateful. In fact, the wealthier one is or aspires to become, the more this attachment grows, causing a reduction in one's ability to savor. You may have heard of studies that show that wealth can increase happiness, but only slightly so."

"I think I've reached that limit."

"I wager that you have. But the good news is, you can begin now—right this moment—to practice being grateful for what you have. Some people even write it down, first thing in the morning, or last thing before bed."

That sounds familiar, Eli thought, before remembering how Angelina had told him she kept a daily gratitude journal. So, there is something to that.

"Of course, there is, Eli," Michael tossed a notebook and fountain pen on the coffee table beside him—where Michael had pulled them from, Eli had no idea.

"Enjoy," Michael winked and promptly disappeared.

CHAPTER TWELVE

THE FUTURE

Eli sat back in his favorite chair, a black leather ottoman in his chic Manhattan apartment. The apartment was one of the homes he owned in major cities around the world, to make his frequent travels feel a little less unfamiliar. He intentionally slammed his head back against the chair, as if attempting to empty the thoughts from his mind. On the footstool before him the morning paper was sprawled out; he had just finished reading articles about Hurricane Harvey and the subsequent flooding in Texas, the massive flooding in South Asia, and a mega storm, Hurricane Irma, now headed towards the Caribbean.

He'd never paid much attention to newspapers before—all they seemed to carry were stories about tragic events. But after his lessons with Michael, he'd begun to seek out information on current events, to consider new perspectives.

A week had passed without any appearance by Michael. Eli was beginning to think his lessons were complete, or perhaps that whole period spent with him was an illusion? Had he dreamed all that? No, he knew those exchanges had happened...he didn't quite know why or how, but they were as real to him as anything else in his life. Perhaps even more real, he thought.

He now had a three-day break from his tour, a welcome and convenient rest from constant activity that allowed him the space needed to process what he'd been learning. The lessons were beginning to make more sense to him, although he still wasn't sure why he had been chosen as Michael's student. He wanted to talk about the shifts in perspective he was undergoing, but who could he talk about them with? His bandmates would think he'd lost his mind…or that he'd become hooked on some hallucinatory drug.

Eli instead took to writing about what he was feeling. Michael had given him a journal, after all. He dedicated one-half to a daily gratitude list, and the other half to notes and reflections and questions he would ask Michael when he returned. If he returns, Eli thought.

"Good morning, Eli."

"Ahh! Why do you do that?!"

"Do what?"

"Appear, out of nowhere like that. Especially when I'm thinking about you."

"Ah, yes. Spirits have a funny way of being called to the source of human thought. Did you know you can do that for anyone? To conjure the spirits of lost loved ones, one must merely place his or her thoughts upon them. Even if they do not appear before you in physical forms, like me, I assure you they are there."

"Well, you scare the shit out of me when you do that. Where have you been?"

"Why, did you miss me?" Michael winked.

"Don't get all touchy-feely. But yes, I suppose I did miss

talking to you. I don't know who else to talk to about all this stuff."

"You can talk to anyone, Eli. But to answer your previous question, I never left. I was merely waiting until you were ready for me to appear before you again. Now, I believe you have some questions for me?"

"Do I ever. Let's start with this article. Hurricane Harvey is devastating Texas right now…scientists are saying that global warming—human-led activity—contributed to making this storm so fatal. Doesn't this bother you?"

Michael stood before Eli, gazing calmly out the window toward the city life below.

"Does it bother you?" Michael echoed Eli's question.

"Yes! Yes, of course, it does! I am not optimistic about the future of humanity, Michael. Climate change is obviously a big problem, and I am disgusted with our government. Please tell me some good news about the world from the way you see it."

"I can't tell you everything, or you will get in your own way, Eli."

Eli rolled his eyes as Michael continued, "But I can tell you that there is hope for your planet and that people like you are volunteering to be here right now to create a necessary shift."

"That sounds like a tall order for one person."

"No one acts alone, Eli. Remember the ripple effect? It takes fewer people than you might think to create systemic change, but it does require a collective elevation in consciousness from those few."

"I wish I could understand all of this better."

"Let me help you," Michael once again placed a hand upon

Eli's head and allowed him to see the future.

It was a future in which humans had learned to adapt to the changing climate rather than trying to control it; a future that adopted new and sustainable economies to replace those that were failing. Advances in technology were embraced that provided every bit of energy needed to run the planet without fossil fuels. The standard of living had been raised for everyone, rather than lowered for many in order to support only a few. Differences in skin color and religion were made obsolete, and using the threat of war to solve problems no longer made sense to anyone. People's love of cooperation had become far greater than the fear that drove them apart.

"It is merely a shift in thinking that makes each of these things possible, Eli. At this moment, you can only imagine what your lives and the world would be like if these strategies were implemented, but I promise you that if you help lead the way, you will be able to see a better place for all of humanity in the future."

Eli threw his arms in the air, "I still can't see how I can make a difference, Michael!"

"You are living in a time when you can expect big things to happen—big shifts in the world and big changes on earth. And just to be clear, the extreme transformations are not only bad things—and they don't need to be good things either, for that matter. You are living the emergence of a new 'normal,' and the success of your transition hinges upon your willingness to acknowledge the shift, and your ability to embrace it healthily."

"So, take climate change, for example. What effects is that going to have on our planet?"

"The crisis of climate change is a perfect example of how

interconnected everything is on your planet: the record-setting droughts caused by shifts in global weather patterns translate directly into scarcity of seasonal crops and the higher prices you pay for food at your local markets. Human activity leading to a warmer climate leads to greater moisture in the atmosphere, and thus greater precipitation and more intense storms such as Hurricane Harvey and Hurricane Irma.

"Do you understand, Eli, that your planet is at the brink of a severe environmental crisis? Issues such as climate change, air and water pollution, waste disposal, deforestation, natural resource depletion, loss of biodiversity…all of these environmental problems require urgent attention."

Eli chuckled smugly, "You're not helping, Michael. You're supposed to be trying to make me feel better."

"I am," Michael smiled as a show of support. "Because here's the good news: These problems can be reversed because Mother Earth is far more powerful than human beings. I am explaining that these are the kinds of extremes in the world that are creating big changes in your lives. Among the many uncertainties that they bring, however, there's one thing that you can be sure of: Lives are changing in ways that you are not used to, not prepared for, and at a speed that you have never known. That is the reason I am here to guide you because we know you are an influencer."

"I'm not here to be an influencer, I'm just here to make people feel good with my music, and that's it."

Michael maintained a patient tone, "Yes, Eli that is true, but there is a whole missing piece that you haven't experienced yet, that we are about to reveal to you."

"Why did you start using, 'we,' Michael? That makes me

nervous…like there's a bunch of aliens out there that are in control of our lives and our planet."

"Well, in a way we are extraterrestrials because we are beings that are from other dimensions. We must teach and guide certain humans when it comes to the huge amount of work that it takes to find their way into the new world that lies ahead of them. I have been having regular dialogues with other souls about you, Eli. We all agree you are nearly ready for the tasks before you.

"Your ability to successfully meet the challenges that are coming in your life begins by acknowledging the issues. Your willingness to focus on your growth and to start asking questions demonstrates your progress. But here's another insight, Eli—this isn't just about you. Everyone on the planet is part of this journey. Your world today is so deeply interconnected on so many levels that it's impossible for the transformation that's emerging in one part not to show up in other places as well. What you put forth in the world can be felt by all you come into contact with. Are you ready to speak of your role in all of this?"

Eli eagerly jumped into the conversation at the same time he jumped from his seat. "Yes! How on earth do I help with all of this?"

"Through the use of sound frequency."

WHAT THE HECK IS THIS GUY TALKING ABOUT? THAT WAS NOT the answer Eli was expecting.

"I thought you were going to tell me my life's purpose."

"Relax, I am about to. Perhaps you will find it interesting that out of the approximately 300 lifetimes you have lived as a human soul, you were a musician 69 times. You understand music like few alive today do, Eli. That is because you know music on a cellular level."

"Ok, so I understand music. So, what?"

"You are to use what you understand, Eli, to help heal the planet."

"That sounds way too big of a responsibility to me."

"You are not the first to be given such responsibility. You have met Carlos Santana once or twice, haven't you? You must be familiar with his declaration that he communicates with an archangel?"

"Yeah, I mean, he was a nice guy, and everything and he sure as hell can play, but that woo-woo stuff? Wasn't that just a result of the use of psychedelics?"

"You tell me, Eli. Is my presence here before you now a result of the use of psychedelics?"

"Ok, you have a point."

"Santana was instructed by his archangel, Metatron, to create the album, Supernatural, using pop culture icons of the day to reach young people—to teach them about the enormous possibilities and opportunities before them."

"Ok, so Supernatural is a great album, but what does it have to do with sound frequency—I mean, how can that heal the planet?"

"That record was put together in such a way that, through sound, it could change the listener's molecular structure. Have you noticed, Eli, how at times you can play one note, and change the entire mood of your audience?"

"Yeah, yeah, I get that," Eli suddenly felt as though pieces of a much larger puzzle were coming together.

"You have done an incredible job of creating music that makes people feel deeply. But you have not channeled that power and responsibility in the best way possible. Much of your music comes from a place of sadness, or even sometimes anger and frustration. What you have the opportunity to do, Eli, is to transform a listener's mood—not merely into a joyful state, but a transcendental state—one in which the listener becomes aware of his or her connection to everyone and everything else in this great universe."

"How exactly do I do that?"

"Through what you know, Eli—through the use of the Fibonacci sequence and the Golden Ratio. This mathematical formula can be used to produce perfect, harmonic healing tones. These tones reconnect one's cellular, emotional, mental and spiritual levels of awareness, or in other words lead listeners to higher states of consciousness."

"How does that work?"

"It's called whole brain synchronization. When the various parts of your brain begin to work together, resonating at the same frequencies and causing neural pathways to fire more rapidly, humans reach intense levels of creativity and clarity. Some of the earth's most brilliant scientists and artists—Einstein, Picasso, Lewis Carol—had high levels of whole brain synchronization. You have touched the tip of the iceberg yourself, Eli, in regard to this practice. But now it is time for you to take this concept much, much further."

"Wow."

"Wow is right. But that's not all. This technique doesn't only lead people to higher states of consciousness and clarity—it heals them, on a cellular level. Your music, using this harmonic tone, expands the chakras within the human species' meridian flow and permeates the muscle structure. It performs a sort of cleansing if you will. Even cancer can be cured when the body starts to resonate at this level of vibration. Do you hear this, Eli? You have the power to heal cancer. If you can do that to the human body, imagine what else you can do for the planet."

"If what you're saying is true, that's pretty incredible."

"Oh, it is very true. But your role goes far beyond making music, Eli."

"How so?"

"Practically every media outlet on your planet is dying to interview you. You have a platform of enormous proportion before you. You can educate the public on what you know— on the lessons we have discussed here together. You are an influencer, Eli, whether you like it or not."

"Michael, that could ruin my career if I talk about this stuff. They'll call me a quack!"

"Or it could elevate the consciousness of the planet. Perhaps it's a risk worth taking, no?"

Eli sighed. "What if I don't want to go through with this?"

"You have no choice."

"But you said I had free will…"

"True, in human form. But you have a karmic history that has to be accounted for—whether you choose to balance it in this life, or in a future life is up to you."

"Karmic history? Now, what are you talking about?"

Michael glanced across the room and asked quietly, "Should I tell him now?"

"What the…? Who are you talking to?"

"Oh. Sorry, I didn't realize I said that out loud. I was just consulting with another guide."

"Jesus…"

"No, not Jesus," Michael joked. "In any case, it has been

agreed. I will tell you more about your previous life as Derek Stryker."

"Please. Enlighten me," Eli inquired coyly.

"You are familiar with the concept of karma, correct?"

"Yeah, I suppose."

"Well, for the sake of clarity, let me give you an overview from the beginning. Karma is the equivalent of Newton's law that 'every action must have a reaction.' Through our thoughts, words, actions, and deeds we deliver a force that must be balanced. No one may escape the consequences of his or her actions.

"Furthermore, what you refuse to accept will continue for you. Therefore, it is true that you have free will—you have the choice to repeat the patterns you have chosen in previous lives. However, to refuse to grow by making different, higher choices, guarantees you the same experience in future lifetimes—what caused you pain in this lifetime will cause you pain in the next.

"And this goes beyond the individual level, Eli. If enough people on the planet choose not to learn from history, history will continue to repeat itself until the corresponding lessons have been learned and a different path has been chosen." Michael paced before the window, his hands linked behind his back, before turning to face Eli directly.

"You made some choices in your last lifetime that need to be balanced."

"What did I do?"

"You did many things as Derek, Eli. One of which was being involved in sex trafficking."

"What?!"

"I don't know that you need to hear the details, Eli, but

many young girls were affected by your decisions.

"Alright, if I buy into this shit, that's pretty bad."

"I would not lie to you, Eli."

"Fuck," Eli pumped his fist in the air in an outburst of anger at himself.

"It is good that you feel what you feel now, Eli. That demonstrates a desire to make choices in this lifetime that are different. Perhaps ones that…don't hurt women, for starters."

"What else did I do?"

"You were a wealthy man, but much of that wealth was accumulated through cheating and misleading others. You were a businessman, and the bottom line always took precedence over the human heart. Colleagues of yours committed suicide, due to decisions you made."

"My God."

"You did not learn to love, Eli. You did not allow yourself to receive love, nor to express it. Your wife and your children suffered greatly as a result."

"Okay, enough already. How do I balance all of that kind of karma?"

"You understand first that you are a participant in the entire universe. You cannot merely be an observer. Do you know that when a human simply looks at a particle that an object consists of—let's say an electron—that electron changes the way it behaves? In fact, the longer we look at it, the more it changes! So, you do understand, then, that you have a role to play in the creation of life on this planet?"

"Yes, I do."

"Good. Just as you refine the music that you play until it meets a certain standard or vision, you may refine—through your deepest beliefs, your words and your actions—the reality of your world. You can rebalance your karma with kindness, compassion, love, and generosity. You may demonstrate these qualities with every interaction, no matter how small, that you have throughout each day. You, Eli, also have the opportunity to demonstrate what you have learned on a massive scale, in the ways we have discussed—through your music and by using your platform. Also, through your wealth.

"Do you remember, Eli, the contract I mentioned you signed as Derek Stryker?"

"Yes."

"Your karmic duty in this lifetime is to earn back the nearly forty billion dollars you left to Gemini—and to use it in service to others."

"Forty billion?! I don't have anywhere close to forty billion."

"You are much closer than you realize, Eli. The remainder will come to you as a result of new business ventures you will embark on in service to others."

"What will I do with all that money, though?"

"That will be your legacy, Eli. You can set up foundations that issue educational scholarships, or grants to charitable organizations. You will have no problem coming up with ways to continue giving, even after the end of your current life.

"I want to talk more about how to use your platform, as well."

"What do you mean by 'platform'?"

"I mean the massive number of people who follow what you do and say. Now, you expressed fear in regard to going public with your newfound understandings. But let me tell you, Eli. You would not be alone. In fact, far from it."

"What do you mean?"

"Many other famous souls are alive on your planet now,

fulfilling their karmic destinies and discussing their spiritual lives in very public ways."

"Like who?"

"Well, I already mentioned Carlos Santana. Alanis Morrisette is another. Aside from musicians, there are also spiritual leaders who are spreading their wisdom through books and films—these names may be unfamiliar to you now, but I assure you they have created massive followings—research Michael Beckwith, Gregg Braden, Deepak Chopra, Debbie Ford, Barbara Marx Hubbard, Marianne Williamson, or Neale Donald Walsch. Tony Robbins is another. All of these leaders and many, many more have developed initiatives to raise the consciousness of people on this planet.

"There are many things you could do to support these initiatives, Eli. You could hold benefit concerts for causes that specifically seek to lead people to higher states of spiritual awareness. You could support politicians—starting even at the local level—that demonstrate a commitment to managing the effects of climate change or another cause you care about. You could write a book about your spiritual growth work, which we are doing together."

"Are you serious?"

"Yes, of course! Why not? Or create a film! Have you seen Tom Shadyac's movie, "Happy?" Tom was an A-list, extremely wealthy movie director who decided to give his wealth away for the benefit of others—because that's what made him happy. Gather with other like-minded, creative people like Tom and see what is possible! When minds that are aligned join together, greater possibility is imagined and achieved. You will be surprised, once you start voicing your beliefs and experiences on the matter, how many others will come forward with a resounding, 'me too!' Even people in your industry. You can be the catalyst, Eli, for people to normalize what has often been brushed aside as 'crazy talk.' You can get people talking…and what's greater, through your music you can get people feeling."

Michael placed a hand upon either of Eli's shoulders, gazing intensely into his eyes. "Are you in?"

Any lingering fear of Eli's was suddenly replaced by excitement. "Yes! Yes, I am in."

CHAPTER THIRTEEN

THE GREATEST POWER

Eli hadn't known exactly what he'd agreed to. However, he knew in his soul he had to follow Michael wherever he led him. As it turned out, that was to the private island in the Bahamas Eli had bought the year before for $20 million and had only vacationed at twice before. The island had survived the brunt of Hurricane Irma, but he was anxious to see his property after the storm.

There wasn't much to his property to start with; the mile-long island was barely developed; Eli's original plan had called for a luxury building to be built amid the island's heavy vegetation, but he never had the time to devote to making further plans. Instead, all that currently stood on the property was a small, two-bedroom cabin. Nevertheless, it functioned properly as a comfortable getaway for his infrequent visits.

"You need a proper vacation," Michael had told him. "Not simply from your career, but from life as you know it. What better place to access inner wisdom than a vacant island, isolated from all the distractions of modern life?"

"Michael, it's going to be hard for me to arrange a vacation of more than a few days. I mean, I'll have to cancel multiple shows in order to be gone for a week or two," Eli had challenged Michael.

"Who said anything about being gone for a week or two? I am talking about a year."

"A year? A whole year? You've got to be joking. You know what my life is like. That would ruin my career."

"There you go again, with this talk of ruining your career. How do you know that such a break wouldn't allow you the opportunity to step back into your career braver, deeper, and more successfully than ever before? Famous musicians like you—Ed Sheeran, Adele, Lady Gaga, to name a few—have done what I am asking you to do, without harming a hair on their head or an album sale."

Eli wanted to continue arguing. The idea was absurd; it would disappoint so many—the fans, his band members, his manager. But he couldn't deny the spark of excitement that had begun to grow inside of him. No media appearances for a year. No interviews, no photo shoots, no...

"Wait! Would there be any women on this island?"

"It's your island, Eli. You can invite whom you want when you want. But I will say that remember, the point of this experience is to limit distractions."

"But..."

"I am not saying sexual energy should be suppressed, Eli—it is natural, and it needs an outlet. But we have studied concepts together brought forth by the writer Napoleon Hill. He had this to say about sexual desire: When men are driven by sexual desire, they develop a level of imagination and creativity unavailable to them at other times. Man can learn, however, to redirect this incredible force and express it instead as art or music or another format that enriches the body, mind, and spirit of man. Doing so can lead one to great heights of achievement. In fact, the one who manages to do so is said to have reached the status of a genius."

"So, no sex for a year?"

Michael laughed, "Again, that is up to you, Eli. I have been a man before, too, and I understand your struggle. But I assure you that if you choose to focus on channeling that valuable source of energy into your transformation, you will find it worth the effort."

I said I am in, Eli had resolved. I will do whatever it takes.

And so, he did. The news was not received warmly by those he had known he would disappoint. To ease any discontent from his manager and band, he generously offered to pay an annual salary to each of them during his absence. To his fans, he promised new, incredible material upon the completion of his sabbatical.

Though he had moments of doubt about his decision, once he arrived on the island he knew he had made the right decision. His cabin was still standing; a few roof tiles had blown off, but otherwise, little damage had been observed. He knew he was luckier than most people living on nearby islands, and he made a personal commitment to financially support those communities as soon as he got settled.

As soon as he threw his bags inside his island home, he felt a deep sense of calm come over him as he had never before experienced. He had no obligations, other than to himself and his growth. He was excited for what this year would offer him.

Michael came in and out of Eli's life throughout the next several months. All Eli had to do to conjure Michael's presence when he needed guidance was to ask for his help. If Eli did not ask for him, Michael left him to his own devices.

When he was called, Michael offered Eli a wide array of tools to help him on his journey.

Michael led Eli in India's ancient technique of Vipassana meditation, where Eli learned to pay disciplined attention to the physical sensations in his body. By doing so, he was able to understand the scientific laws that operated his thoughts, feelings, and judgments and, therefore, begin to free himself from any latent idea of suffering.

Michael taught Reiki to Eli, the Japanese technique that promotes healing by laying one's hands upon another to help increase his or her life force energy. As a patient of Michael's, Eli experienced deep relaxation and feelings of peace, security, and wellbeing. "I can't wait to offer this to someone else," Eli told Michael after his first session. "Preferably a woman," he added with a grin.

In addition to the healing of Eli's mind and spirit, he underwent a disciplined physical transformation. Michael encouraged him to undergo several natural detoxification processes. "Let's have you start with a liver cleanse, Eli. After all your years on the road—combined with your exposure to toxins in food, air, water, and the environment—you must certainly be in need of one."

Anything Eli needed, he had delivered by boat from Nassau; he simply sent word via e-mail to the local personal assistant he had hired, and she arranged the shopping and delivery. He was pleased with the woman's professionalism and the privacy she afforded him; not once did she ask what such items as wheat grass, dandelion greens, wormwood, and black walnut hull were to be used for. He didn't know himself—he passed all of the ingredients Michael had suggested over to the personal chef he had hired, who made daily deliveries of juices, tea infusions and vegetarian meals to the island.

Eli had had to make major changes to his diet. Michael instructed him to remove all foods containing sugars and all refined flour and wheat products from his meals. "What the hell can I eat?" Eli had moaned at first, but once his body started feeling refreshed and energized, he accepted the changes without regret. He even began running—a sport he had previously despised—every morning, making five loops around the island.

"You know, Michael, I'm beginning to realize that if I had continued at the pace I was at for the last several years, I probably would have developed cancer or some other disease…my body feels so different now. I never imagined it was possible to feel this good."

"That's how the body was made to feel, Eli. Many humans have lost touch completely with how it feels to be healthy— how it is supposed to feel to be human."

After nine months on the island, Michael was pleased with Eli's mental, physical, and spiritual progress. He had worked through all and any emotional blocks from his childhood which, even with the most wonderful parents there were some energies transferred from the history of his own parents and their ancestors.

"You know, Eli, I have noticed something significantly different about you."

"So much is different about me, Michael. Everything."

"I am glad you are aware of your transformation. You have assimilated your lessons more rapidly than I had expected."

"I am glad you had such high faith in me," Eli winked.

"If I had not had high faith in you from the start, Eli, I

would never have bothered teaching you."

"Thank you, Michael. I mean it…for everything."

"You need not thank me, Eli. If you wish to express gratitude, there are two other people who would be most appreciative to hear those words."

Two other people. Eli did not have to think long to understand who Michael was speaking of.

"My parents."

"Indeed, Eli. Have you considered inviting them to the island? You have not been in contact with them since you told them of your plans to come here. Parents never stop worrying about their children, you know."

"I've thought about them. Often, in fact. They would probably hardly recognize me now."

"I believe the surprise would be a pleasant one."

Eli smiled, "I agree."

ROBERT AND CAROL HAD JUMPED AT THE CHANCE TO VISIT their son. His call alone had nearly shocked them—not just the fact that he called, but that his voice sounded calm and patient. He did not speak of having somewhere else he needed to be.

It was their first time in the Bahamas, and it was a far cry from their farm in Brownsville. However, they were pleased by the modesty of the property; they felt comfortable there.

"It's beautiful, Eli," his mother had exclaimed after having disembarked from the boat and given her son the longest hug she had been allowed to give him in years. "I see why you've spent so much time here this year."

"I came here not just because it's beautiful, Mom. I came here to get away from it all— the fame, the ego, materialism, the distractions from…my life's purpose."

"It's nice to hear you talk this way, son," Eli's dad chimed in.

"it's nice just to talk to you," his mother added.

"I know I haven't been the best son these past several years. I am sorry I have been so absent. I know I must have hurt you both." Eli's parents remained silent, but he noticed the tears welling up in his mother's eyes as he continued, "I want you to know, though, that I understand now…how much you sacrificed for me…how much you taught me, simply by example. Thank you for everything you have done for me."

"We raised you with pleasure, Eli," his mother began. "Even when you left us, we knew you would return to us one day. When you were ready. You were a special boy, and we knew you'd grow into being the incredible man you were capable of being."

"I don't know if I'm 'him' yet, honestly. I feel like my journey into manhood is just beginning. But I'm full of ideas and goals and visions about how to make a great contribution to the planet—not just through playing music, but through philanthropy. And that's not all either…through loving like I've never loved before. And that starts with you both, Mom and Dad. I love you."

"We love you, son. More than you can imagine," Eli's dad was crying now, too. It occurred to Eli that his parents no longer seemed so "simple." He now noticed a depth to them he'd never paused to discover before. Neither of his parents had ever been afraid to show their emotions. It used to embarrass him, but now he admired them for that quality with deep appreciation. How many times had they demonstrated unconditional love and forgiveness? And patience, and generosity? What great teachers I had, right under my nose, Eli thought.

"You know, for the longest time, I felt you were…disappointed in me. In how I lived my life…" Eli was feeling emotional himself; this time, he refused to hold back the tears that were forming in his own eyes at the depth of those words and the wounds they'd formed over the years.

"You never disappointed us, Eli. Not once," his mother answered. "We knew you were simply following your life's path."

Eli could feel the honesty in his mother's voice. He looked at his dad and felt his agreement. What a fool I've been, he thought. Weight was lifted off of him that he hadn't known had been so heavy.

ELI'S PARENTS STAYED ON THE ISLAND FOR JUST OVER A WEEK. The three filled their days by going for walks, reading books and resting in the hammocks. Their nights were filled with board games, campfire songs, and thoughtful conversations. They had years to catch up on. Eli got to know his parents not just as Mom and Dad but as Carol and Robert.

Long forgotten memories from his youth flooded back to him; his mom would point out medicinal plants that grew on the island, and Eli would recall how she had done the same on the farm. Carol shared family stories with him, about her Aunt Maggie and lessons she had learned from her time spent with members of native tribes.

It became clear to Eli that his parents understood the interconnectedness of all things. Perhaps that is why, in the end, Eli was willing to accept the lessons Michael taught him—it felt like they were lessons he already knew. If you remove the ego, the truth is revealed, he determined.

He was sad when it came time for his parents to leave the island. "The farm needs tending," his father had said. Eli recognized that his work ethic and drive had come from his father. My musical interests came from my parents, too, he thought. So much of me is a product of them.

Eli hadn't told his parents about Michael...directly, anyway. They had asked their son who or what was responsible for his transformation, but he had answered simply, "I have had many teachers along the way, who all entered my life at the exact moment that I needed them. In fact, some I didn't recognize as teachers until much later."

"Are you planning on going back to music, son?" his father asked.

"Music, yes, of course. I have a lot of new material I've been working on recently, and I'm anxious to share it with the fans. But..." Eli's confidence gave way to a growing sense of vulnerability. "I'm not sure how it will be received. How I will be received. The messages I'm going to share will be rather...different than before. So much of what I used to sing about feels frivolous to me now. I hope my fans will welcome the shift."

"Those who are ready to follow you in the direction you are going will do so."

"I suppose that is true."

"I'm very proud of you, son."

"And so am I," Carol added, placing a kiss on Eli's cheek.

Eli hugged his mother, then looked contemplatively off into the distance. "My life will get very busy again soon."

"What is important is just that you don't lose yourself in that busy-ness. If your actions are aligned with your purpose, they will invigorate you rather than burn you out," his mom advised.

"Hey, if I ever fall back into that pattern of not calling you or answering your calls...please come and kick my ass, will you?" Eli grinned.

"All the way to Timbuktu," his mother joked.

I have to love their corniness, Eli thought to himself with a smile, as he watched his parents board the boat that would take them to the airport in Nassau and from there back home to Brownsville, Oregon.

For the remaining three months of Eli's sabbatical, he wrote and wrote until he filled seven notebooks with new song material—all written within a frequency that would open people's hearts, and with lyrics that he hoped would expand people's minds and spirits. He also spent countless hours teaching himself how to play the sitar—he would incorporate the instrument into his new album.

Now, he was even listening to popular music with a whole new perspective; songs he'd heard on the radio, such as Jason Mraz's Everything is Sound, and I Won't Give Up revealed to him just how many other musicians out there shared his newly discovered spiritual beliefs.

Where was I all these years? What took me so long? Eli questioned, but without shame. I guess I just wasn't ready. Eli read about Mraz's raw vegan diet and the entertainer's investment in Los Angeles's Café Gratitude. Furthermore, the singer was passionately working towards educating people about the effects of climate change.

Eli had his ideas for new business ventures that he predicted would not only turn profits but would contribute to the health of the people and the planet. As he explored ways to offer hope to humanity, he became amazed at the number of people out there doing similar, meaningful work. Jon Bon Jovi, for example, created a nonprofit organization to fight poverty "one soul at a time." The organization helped provide more than 500 affordable homes for those in need and even opened a community restaurant called JBJ Soul Kitchen, which Eli read serves everyone regardless of their ability to pay. The model operates on a pay-it-forward basis—customers either volunteer for their meal or dine and pay for a meal for someone else.

I could open a whole chain of restaurants all over the world using such a model, Eli thought. Through his research, he learned about organizations such as Thriive, which provides donor-funded loans to small business entrepreneurs in developing nations which, instead of being repaid to the organization, are "paid forward" in the donation of services, products or job training to other small business entrepreneurs.

The model appeared to be working—one of Thriive's loans, for example, paid for a woman to purchase industrial sewing equipment, which she repaid by creating and donating life-vest backpacks to students from poor, flood-prone areas of Vietnam. The development of her business also provided jobs for thirty women. Very few of the loans aren't paid back since, according to the organization, the entrepreneurs are so inspired by the impact their gifts have on their communities that 72% of them continue to give years after having received financial support.

Brilliant! Eli thought. Eli suddenly felt like he had the whole world open up to him, in an entirely different way than the one he'd lived merely through touring. I can pick any topic of interest—anything, Eli thought, and invest in educating myself and subsequently educating and serving others. What will the causes I select be? He wondered with excitement.

To say that Eli left his island in the Bahamas with a renewed sense of spirit would be an understatement. He practically floated off the island. He felt at a peak state of mental, physical, and spiritual health, but he also was more than ready to return to "civilization."

He had grown lonely—over the past month in particular. Michael hadn't been around much, which of course was due to his lack of need. And to be honest, he was eagerly anticipating having women around once again.

Eli had been in touch with his manager a few weeks before his planned return. "Notify the band, please. I'm ready to begin working again," he had proudly declared. "And tell the guys to be ready—I have a shitload of new material for them to learn," he grinned. "And maybe even some new instruments."

Arrangements were made for him to meet them all in L.A. for what would turn into several weeks of intense rehearsals and recording sessions. To Eli's delight, the band was pleasantly surprised by his new music.

"These songs are like your previous hits, on crack," Jimbo had said.

"This stuff makes me want to shit my pants, man. It's so fucking good," Mark added.

I forgot what it's like to be with the guys, Eli laughed to himself. It was good to be back. Now I just need to find a balance between road life and this new version of me.

Returning to the hustle of Los Angeles had felt like culture shock to Eli; he had forgotten just how noisy and polluted the city was. His first two days back, he didn't leave his apartment. He was too overstimulated—and repulsed, honestly, by how distracted everyone was. Where are they all hurrying off to? What can possibly be so important? He realized that had been him, not too long ago. He was determined not to fall into that pattern again; he would build time into his schedule to rest and to maintain his newly acquired meditation practice.

The band didn't buy into his new routine as readily as they did his new music. However, Eli could sense the guys' curiosity as to how he'd not only written such killer material but how he'd managed to convert himself into a much calmer, at-peace person. They joked that he must have done ayahuasca or some other drug, but he assured him his transformation was completely natural.

"I studied with a great teacher," he shared.

Two months after his return, the new album was ready to be released. Great hype had been built; Russ made sure all of the major media outlets knew that something extraordinary was about to come out of Eli—not just by way of music, but through business ventures, philanthropy, and a new message he wanted to share with the masses.

A new tour was about to kick off in promotion of the new album. The opening concert would be held in New York at Madison Square Garden. It was a night Eli had envisioned in his mind many times during his year on the island. What is the core of my message? He'd asked himself. What do I want to share with the fans about my transformation?

The night of the concert, he felt more nervous than he'd ever been before going on stage. He experienced moments of doubt, what if they don't like the new material? What if my message is misinterpreted, or written off as woo-woo? Michael's—and his father's words—came back to him, however. Those who are ready to follow you in the direction you are going will do so.

In fact, his parents were in the audience tonight. Eli had not only invited them this time but emphasized how important it was to him that they be at this show. He'd flown them out to New York the day before, and had made certain he had time to have dinner with them before meeting with his band to go over last-minute details of their upcoming tour. He'd even had his parents stay with him at his Manhattan apartment.

Finally, the moment arrived. The stage had been newly arranged after the opening band left the stage, and the crowd was already chanting, "Eli! Eli! Eli!" It felt good to know that, so far anyway, the sabbatical didn't seem to have hurt his career.

Eli took a deep breath. *We've got this.* Confidently, he walked out on stage to roaring applause. Signs were everywhere, and he took the time to read a few, "Good to have you back, Eli!" "We missed you!" and the ever-present, "We love you, Eli!"

Eli felt the love. His eyes welled up with tears, and this time he wasn't afraid to show it. He took his place at the microphone and shared, "Wow, you guys. I'm touched. Truly. Thank you for being here tonight, thank you for staying with me even when I was gone. It means the world to me."

"Your music means the world to us, Eli!" a fan cried out from the front row.

"Thank you, thank you. You guys are awesome. Now, I want to share something with you all about where I've been, or rather what I've gone through over the past year. A…special friend…helped guide me through some revelations. I had been living a rather purpose-less life. I mean, I made music that many people resonated with, but I wasn't reaching my highest potential.

"Music is actually a lot more powerful than even I realized. I have been blessed to have been given a voice and a talent that can be used to not only reconnect people to their spirits but to spread a message that people on our planet so desperately need to hear these days. I hope that, as you listen to the new music we've put together for you, you let the harmonies and the lyrics sink into your hearts. Or rather, open your hearts… because love is the greatest power."

Eli deliberately made eye contact with his parents, who were in the front row. A moment later, a slight movement off to the side of the stage caught Eli's attention. A quick glance proved to him what he'd already felt; Michael was standing there, with a big grin on his face. Eli nodded at him with a smile, before bending down to pick up his guitar and kick off his set.

The night was magical. Though Eli interspersed some of his earlier hit songs into the set, the majority of the material was new and at a frequency that would elevate the listener's consciousness—whether they were aware of it, or not. Eli incorporated the sitar into a few of his rock songs, and his band contributed the instruments of tabla and tambura. Eli even chanted at certain times, to the tune of "om." For Eli, and even his band members, the result was a spiritual experience. He felt strongly that his fans felt it, too. *We are really onto something here,* Eli beamed.

Petra Nicoll

THE PRESS WENT CRAZY AFTER THAT GIG; HE'D NEVER RECEIVED so much publicity. The reviews were mostly positive, but some questioned Eli's new direction. "Has Eli Evans gone off his rocker?" one tabloid headlined. Some accused him of being high when he wrote and performed his songs, whereas others applauded his courage and innovation. Overall, however, his return to the stage was welcomed and congratulated.

Over time, he began to share more about the transformation he experienced while in interviews. In fact, if he agreed to an interview, he insisted on being asked questions that actually mattered. "I want to talk about living a life of purpose," he shared. "I don't want to just talk about myself. Let's talk about what every one of us can do to contribute to a more loving and sustainable planet."

He introduced concepts Michael had taught him in his lessons. He shared healing techniques he'd learned while on sabbatical in the Bahamas. Eli's following began to expand; he lost some of the earlier fans, but he no longer feared that result. In fact, he recognized that fear, in fact, was likely what kept those fans from being open to what he had to share. For every fan lost, two were gained…simply by being authentic and open.

Eli ended up cutting ties with some of the brands he'd previously had contracts with. He chose instead to collaborate with companies whose missions he believed in. He became a spokesperson for TOMS shoes, which for every pair of shoes sold donates another to those in need. He was also in the process of developing his clothing line, which would donate an article of clothing to a homeless person in Los Angeles with every purchase. He had a vision of expanding the model to serve every city around the country, and later the globe, but he wanted to start with where he was based.

Charity events were being planned to support what had become some of his key chosen causes—namely global warming and human trafficking. Anytime a disaster was to strike—a hurricane, a flood, a fire—Eli organized a fundraising initiative to support those affected. "We're in this together," he would always say.

Eli knew he had barely scratched the surface of all he now wanted to accomplish in his life. "I thought I had been to the mountaintop," he reflected. "I had merely reached the first base camp."

Eli had also been successful at scheduling time off during his tours. He didn't hit as many cities or participate in as many media appearances, but those choices didn't affect his success. In fact, the work-life balance he was able to achieve allowed him to be more present and perform his absolute best each time he hit the stage.

Sometimes, he indulged in entertainment that wasn't even music or job-related. Such was the case when he'd noticed an ad in the entertainment paper for the Awareness Film Festival—a fundraiser for an organization called Heal One World. The name would never have attracted his attention or interest in the past, but now it made him curious. It was the final day of the festival, and a film about the caste system in India was going to be shown. Apparently, the film had attracted the attention of some industry bigwigs and was touted as a possible contestant at the Cannes Film Festival.

What the heck, I'll go, he decided. Eli figured it was an obscure event where he might be able to blend into the crowd a bit. Nevertheless, he dressed in a nice suit and tie; it was

Hollywood after all, and the media might be in attendance at a film festival. Catching himself in the mirror before he left his Santa Monica suite, he was pleased with his appearance. I look younger than I did a year ago, he noticed with pleasure.

He hadn't driven much at all over the past year, and it was a pleasure to settle into the driver's seat of his Aston Martin. He had become accustomed to a simpler life while on the island and had felt a draw toward returning to a more minimalistic lifestyle in the States. In some ways, he'd succeeded, but he did still enjoy a luxury car.

As he wove through the streets of Los Angeles's suburbs, he had an eerie feeling that he'd been there before—in that exact place, in those exact circumstances. It felt like déjà vu, only deeper. He'd had such experiences more and more lately; sometimes he had dreams, in fact, that bore striking similarities to future events. He interpreted those experiences as indications that he was still on his path. I am meant to be at this festival tonight, he thought.

It took him half an hour to arrive and park near the theater. He was surprised to find more guests in attendance than expected. Maybe there are more people awakening now than I thought. He eased over to the ticket booth, careful to avoid the red carpet that had been laid out and the press that lined up beside it. He had arrived late for the grand entrance, but a few people were still trickling in.

"One ticket for The People on the Other Side, please."

"I'm sorry sir, but tickets have been sold out for over a week. Guest list only," the ticket attendant didn't even look up at him.

Eli's disappointment was not hard to hide. "What? But it was in this week's entertainment paper..."

"We sold out just after press time. I'm sorry, but if you are not on the guest list, we'll need to ask you to step aside. There are others waiting, and the film is just about to begin," the cashier glanced up from the paperwork in front of her just long enough to recognize who stood before her.

"Oh! I am very sorry, Mr. Evans. We will make an exception for you. Please, go on into the theater. I will notify the door attendant."

Being famous does have its perks, Eli thought as he made his way into the theater. A few photos of him were snapped on his way in; the paparazzi would be ever-present in his life, he accepted. The lights had already been dimmed, so he made his way to the first of the few available seats he spotted, in the very back row.

The opening credits had already scrolled, and the film was now beginning with a scene in Dharavi, one of the world's largest slums, located in Mumbai, India. The images devastated Eli's heart; to see children, especially, living amid such an abundance of trash and lack of necessary resources moved him to tears.

What can I do about this? He immediately started contemplating. Just as his imagination began to run wild with ways to support an initiative for India, his emotions were taken for a ride once again. There, magnified on the large screen before him, were the most beautiful eyes he had ever seen. They were peering into a child's eyes, and they were unmistakably the eyes he had once lovingly peered into himself.

I can't believe it; he whispered under his breath as his heart dropped into his chest. The image expanded and revealed the full body of the woman, adorning a sari and reaffirming who Eli had known those eyes to belong to. Angelina. He sat motionless, staring at the screen in awe.

Why am I so surprised? I knew she had it in her. His mind raced with questions. Does she live in Los Angeles now? Is she here tonight? Oh God, will I see her? If I see her, what will I say? Will she even want to talk to me?

He became aware now, more than ever, of all of the things he wanted to say to her. He wanted to tell her about the amazing journey he'd been on over the past year. He wanted to tell her all about Michael—he knew that she, of all people, would not think he was crazy. He wanted to tell her he had discovered his life's purpose. She will understand.

For the next ninety minutes, he sat just enough engaged in the film to follow the story and admire Angelina's acting, but at the same time, he ran possible scenarios through his head about having the opportunity to reach out to her.

His heart started beating faster at the end of the film when it was announced that there would be a Q&A with members of the cast and crew for those who wished to stick around. The audience gave a standing ovation as, third to enter from stage left, was Angelina. He observed that no one left; everyone in attendance stayed, and a line began forming at a microphone to ask questions.

Eli's nerves grew as he realized the opportunity before him. Should I get in line? He would have much preferred a private moment with Angelina, but with a crowd this size and the degree of attention she was receiving, he feared he wouldn't be able to access that moment. It's now or never, Eli decided. He took his place at the end of the line.

Waiting patiently through question and answer, question

and answer, Eli mulled over what he would ask. He couldn't believe his luck when, just as it was finally his turn to step up to the microphone, the host announced, "Thank you, everyone. This has been a wonderful evening, and we do so appreciate your interest in this remarkable film, but we must close questioning at this time."

A moan rang out from those that remained in line behind him, and Eli stood frozen in disbelief. His eyes, however, had managed to lock with Angelina's. She stood frozen, as well. It took a moment before her wits were regained and she leaned forward into the microphone that had been set up before her.

"Pardon me, Sharon, thank you for keeping this event on track so well, but I do have time for one more question."

Sharon looked confused but obliged to Angelina's request. "Certainly, go ahead, sir," she turned to Eli.

"Thank you, yes, I…was just wondering…what your plans are for later."

All eyes were on Eli; he could hear people murmuring among the audience, "That's Eli Evans!"

Angelina remained calm and politely replied, "I am not able to reveal details yet, but I do have a special film project in the works. It's a screenplay I wrote, in fact."

Eli suddenly felt emboldened, "That's wonderful. I look forward to that immensely. But I was referring to your plans for tonight."

A giggle spread across the audience, in eager anticipation of Angelina's reply.

"Well, in fact, I will be catching up with a dear friend," she paused, and her smile left no room for doubt about who that friend would be.

Eli's attention was elsewhere, of course, but had he bothered to turn around at that moment; he would have seen Michael lingering in the back of the room, with a look of smug satisfaction on his face. "Let the show begin," he said aloud, but no one was able to hear him.

1) Free Will
2) unconditional Love / compassion

3) Purpose
4) Know Theyself / what's in yr memory cells
5) giving + receuing / bed service
6) Gratitude

166 -   2 lessons
        (1) Free will
167   (2) illusion + unconditional love

170 #3 Meditation healing old stories
        Love Hate, Fear
174
175   Lack of purpose, pleasure + control
176   What is our greatest purpose
178 Change negative thought to
                        positive
78 Knowing theyself at a soul
                            level
179 Need access to what is programed
     into your memory + cellular
     levels from past life times

180 What is my purpose
181 lessa (5) giving and receiving
        being of service
184 lessa #6 gratitude

Made in the
USA
Lexington, KY